Delphine Dodd

Delphine Dodd

by

S.P. Miskowski

Omnium Gatherum
Los Angeles CA

Delphine Dodd

ISBN-13: 978-0615698182
ISBN-10: 0615698182

http://omniumgatherumedia.com

This book is a work of fiction. Names, characters, places, and
incidents either are the products of the author's imagination or are
used fictitiously, and any resemblance to actual events or persons,
living or dead, is entirely coincidental.

First Edition

Advance Praise for Delphine Dodd

"Along with Brendan Connell's *The Architect*, I rate *Delphine Dodd* as the best novella I read in 2012." —Peter Tennant, *Black Static*

"Delphine Dodd not only expands and illuminates the tragedy in the brilliant novel, Knock Knock, but also further proves Miskowski possesses that talent most enviable in a writer: she makes you BELIEVE." —Simon Strantzas, author of *Nightingale Songs*

"Miskowski doesn't merely craft 'atmosphere,' she generates gravity. Dark and compelling, Delphine Dodd is a singularity... pick it up and its pull is inescapable." — Ennis Drake, author of *Twenty-Eight Teeth of Rage*

"The fantastical world of Skillute, Washington, first masterfully plumbed in the Omnium Gatherum Media release (Shirley Jackson Award nominee and finalist) Knock Knock is revisited in S.P. Miskowski's Delphine Dodd, the first in a proposed series of three novellas set in the shadowy wonderworld of the Pacific Northwest... The characters are fascinating and exhibit a rare, well-drawn depth. Miskowski does an extraordinary job of drawing the reader into the past and into the lives of her characters. This novella works well as a stand alone read, but once you are drawn into S.P. Miskowski's darkly magical world, you will feel the thirst to explore it in depth." —Walt Hicks, *Hellbound Times*

For Matthew Scott Olson

Over the River and Through the Woods

The crows acted like they owned the place. They didn't lift a wing to fly. They hopped and paced from branch to branch, casting shadows along deeper shadows in the cedars. They cawed to signal one another: Look here, a sight to see! Two of the feathered monsters, black eyes sparkling in the failing light, were bold enough to perch on a mound of earth on the other side of the narrow road, staring at us.

"How come they look at us like that?" Olive asked me.

"Don't be scared," I told her. "We probably woke them up. They're just curious."

I didn't know if this was true. I didn't know what a dozen crows might do on the spur of the moment. But, Olive was only eight, two-and-a-half years younger than me. So I thought I ought to say it. One of the birds, a fat sleek fellow balanced on a maple branch, cocked his head to the side and opened his beak wide but didn't make a sound.

"I'm not scared," said Olive.

Brave girl. Not very clever, but she had a stout heart.

Considering the hour and the amount of travel time, I decided we must be inland just north of the Columbia, and probably shy of the Cowlitz. I had dozed off during the last leg of our journey. When I woke up it was over. We had crossed the river by barge or by bridge, and I'd slept through it. I kicked myself for that. Now I couldn't tell for sure how many miles north of the Columbia we were. But we were certainly in Washington. Night was coming on fast. We would have reached the south side of the river long before nightfall.

What I knew for certain was that we were in a forest and it was after dusk. So we waited uncertain and quiet by the side of the road, ogled by inquisitive crows.

In those days I had long hair, which was black like my mother's and matched my eyes. I wore it in a braid with a blue silk ribbon. My dress was buttoned up close to the chin and I wore my coat for most of the trip. I felt better that way, especially when Mama made me sit next to John Dee while he drove. He had conducted this journey as he usually did, half-drunk and overconfident after a sleepover in a ratty, seaside hotel. But this time, instead of returning south to the rooming house in Eugene, he had driven us to this spot somewhere in the woods north of the Columbia River.

That day Mama had taken the front passenger seat and barely looked at us girls. I wondered why she was so quiet. She had stopped flouncing in her new silk dress and complaining that it wasn't made for travel. She had stopped laughing. Her black bob was tucked smartly under a white scarf, and her lips were painted crimson. The fox stole John Dee had rescued from our landlady rested on Mama's left shoulder wearing a hopeless expression.

For most of the previous day she had sat in back with Olive and pointed out 'landmarks of interest.' All in the high, cheerful voice she took on whenever she started drinking John Dee's blackberry wine.

We had pursued bumpy, winding roads along the coast because Mama said the trip ought to be 'special and scenic.' We had stopped to admire the picked-over wreckage of the *Peter Iredale*, a barque driven ashore a few years earlier and trapped in the sand, her mighty masts hanging to one side, rotting away. As John Dee drove us east and away from the ocean, we had spotted warehouses and canneries where the workers packed salmon and sturgeon. We had seen enormous wooden fish wheels on the river, and John Dee remarked:

"Now there's the smart way to catch a salmon. Only a damn fool would hunt fish with a canoe."

When he said this he reached over and pinched Mama, who pushed his hand away. By then she had helped herself to a good supply of wine and was beginning to wind down and sulk. Olive took the opportunity to start singing an opera she had made up on the spot, until she caught a withering look from John Dee and decided to quiet down.

My sister was lighter than me, lighter in her skin and hair and eyes, but also her voice. She had what people called a musical voice. She was pretty but sort of soft and pudgy. She smiled too much, I thought, even when there was no reason to smile. I used to ask her, sometimes, what she was smiling about, but she would only shake her head and laugh. That made me mad. I still don't know why.

It had been a long trip. Two days of off-and-on drizzle and the usual mechanical trouble. Now my sister and I stood in the darkening border between the woods and the road, holding hands, waiting. Everything could change in a minute. We knew that well enough. Mama might shout out for John Dee to turn around. She might come back to fetch us, and swear that she would never leave again. This had happened twice the year before, in Portland and then Astoria.

The toes of our battered shoes lined up roughly along the edge of moss spreading to meet the muddy road. The night rain cast its sheen across the outer forest, trapping spots of moonlight in puddles. They glowed like paper lanterns between the ferns and cedars.

From the spot where we stood, the dirt road climbed gradually away. Then it snaked to the left and continued uphill. I couldn't see it any more but nearly a quarter of a mile off the automobile rattled its way into the night. The machine was a Tin Lizzie. Mama called it the Contraption. For weeks she had tried to wheedle the promise of a better vehicle out of John Dee. She had her heart set on something called a Crane Simplex, but I figured she would never get one, at least not to keep. John Dee and his friends were lowdown criminals, more talk than cash. Their money came and went like water.

Even after the sound of the Tin Lizzie died away, we waited. Finally Olive spoke.

"Is she coming back?"

"No," I said. Might as well admit the truth and let it bleed out. "Not this time."

Olive didn't cry. She never cried. She looked at me. I knew that if I showed no fear my sister would gladly stare down a rabid wolf. And who knew? There might be wolves in this place. There were plenty of crows. Wherever this place was, strung together out of moss and mud, scattershot with red alder and dogwood. Olive started to shiver so I put my arm around her shoulders.

Earlier that afternoon we had passed a clearing where the rippling light of the river had barely shown through the trees. John Dee had pulled over and stopped to relieve himself on a boulder. I marveled at that man's inability to simply pee on the ground like the other men Mama had known. He would hold out until he spied a tree or a rock or a fence he liked, and then he would announce his intentions and pull over, making a kind of ceremony out of the whole thing.

"Them girls don't know how lucky they are," he said over his shoulder to Mama as soon as he was done, because another part of the ceremony was to make conversation after the fact, while buttoning his trousers.

"That's enough," Mama told him. She sounded drowsy and far away.

"Listen, now," said John Dee. "Did you girls know your granny lives right down the road from a famous site?"

"You want to relieve yourself on that, too?" Mama asked.

John Dee never laughed at Mama's jokes, and this time was no exception. He finished buttoning up with one foot on the running board, and said to Olive:

"If your mama had stayed put she might've married herself a Kanaka and you'd be asleep in a little wigwam tonight, snug as a bug."

Mama had laughed then, a small snort that meant what he'd said was stupid but she didn't have the nerve to tell him outright. She played with the tiny blue silk purse she always wore around her neck. John Dee turned to me and said:

"Better say your prayers every night, little girl."

"Why?" I asked him point blank because I was sleepy and not thinking straight.

"So the river spooks don't get you, when they come creeping through the night. They crawl up from the river like Southern catfish, them Kanakas, crawl out of the water on their elbows, with mud all over their faces."

"There's no Kanaka around here," Mama said. And then she mumbled: "It's not even a Chinook word."

John Dee fixed his eyes upon her. This was the look that said they'd have words later.

Mama had stopped pointing out landmarks after that. Maybe she was too tired, too worn down by these men like John Dee who paid our way for months at a time. But in the years that followed I sometimes liked to think maybe she had a tiny regret, for her daughters, for the place where she was leaving us, even for the life she'd once led there herself.

In the end, all we had to do was turn around. Our grandmother's house stood only a hundred feet away, flanked by fir trees so tall we couldn't see the uppermost branches. The plank house was hoary, its walls weathered to green-blue and speckled with moss. We stared in the window like hungry cats. Inside, a cast iron stove gave off a glow all the way from the kitchen, inviting us away from the road, out of the night air and the spring rain and the calling of crows in the trees.

I hoisted the cloth satchel on my shoulder. The surface

was damp. Everything we owned was packed into this small case, including the shortbread Mama had wrapped in a stained, embroidered table napkin she'd stolen from the last hotel.

We didn't have to knock. The front door, fashioned from soft wood and sporting weeds in the crevices, swung open before us. Into its frame stepped a figure unlike anyone I'd ever seen. For a second I imagined that the broad-shouldered woman with blue eyes and dark complexion had also grown from the mottled door.

Her dress was brown and she wore a faded cotton apron over it. The apron was stained with splotches of crimson, indigo, and emerald. Her shoes were slippers made of tanned deer hide. Around her neck she wore a tiny leather sack with a drawstring. On a ribbon she wore a single key made of dull brass. She was wiping blood from her hands with a damp cloth.

We stared at her face. Then we stared at her hands. Finally the woman looked down and said:

"Chicken. I'm cleaning chicken for tomorrow's supper."

Being the elder I took it upon myself to close my mouth, which I'd suddenly realized was slack. It was my job to make the introductions. Little sister still gaped.

"I'm Delphine, and this is Olive." I leaned in close to Olive and whispered: "Livvy, shut your mouth."

Olive obeyed so quickly that she made a clicking sound when her teeth met. She was still staring, and she looked like she might scream. Instead she asked:

"Are you Granny?"

The woman cracked a smile, deepening the lines in her face. She had fine white teeth and a dimple in her chin exactly like Mama's.

"You call me Eve Alice," she told us.

"You're not our grandma?" Olive asked, and I had to jab her in the ribs, prompting a grunt.

"Eve Alice is fine for now," the woman said again and looked at her hands. "Chicken for supper tomorrow. Soup tonight."

She held the door open wide and we entered.

Late that night, our bellies full of salmon chowder and biscuits, we lay side by side in the pitch dark of the room upstairs listening to the house groan. Everything was old: the wide floorboards, the bed, and the cedar rafters. Yet it all seemed perfectly made for us.

If Eve Alice knew we were coming to stay, she never said so. She opened her house and let us inside. Our room was waiting, and it was as cozy as she could make it. The curtains were indigo, and so were the shutters outside our windows. Our bed was as wide as it was long, framed by stout bedposts carved into black birds.

"Crows," Olive said.

"Ravens," Eve Alice corrected.

The huge carved birds huddled with their claws tucked beneath them, eyes closed. Each one faced a different direction.

Once we were settled on the goose-down mattress Eve Alice had piled layer after layer of patchwork quilts on top of us. In the end we were buried beneath a tapestry of crimson and gold with a cream border. To move an arm or a leg took a determined effort.

"We have rules," Eve Alice told us. "Don't fall down the stairs and break your neck. Don't go into the woods to the outhouse at night."

"Are there wolves out there?" Asked Olive.

"Wolves, coyotes, bears..."

"Do you carry a rifle?" I asked.

"No need," said Eve Alice. "I know the woods. But you stay in the house at night. Keep a pot under your bed. Clean up in the morning. If you ever get sick in the night, call out and I'll come."

She placed a ceramic bowl on the floor on each side, one for me and one for Olive. After she shuttered the lantern and climbed down the winding flight of stairs, after the creaks and groans of the house faded away, I lay awake, blinking in the dark, listening to the mild snoring of my sister. I was surprised that I didn't cry then. Not crying made me feel a little sad.

Mama was far away by now. Did she miss us? There was an ache in my chest, not sharp but persistent like the dull throb of a toothache. I missed the dark glimmer of Mama's hair, and the perfume she bought in a red glass bottle at the five and ten in Eugene. I missed her black, thick eyelashes and the way she smiled when John Dee wasn't watching her. Mama's natural smile was sly, and sometimes mean.

All of a sudden I was longing to see these things, but in some way I could never admit back then, I knew we were better off with Eve Alice. Strange as it was, I knew I could sleep through the night here. I'd never done that before in the long journey we'd taken from grand hotel to cheap hotel to a shared parlor in a rooming house to the back corner of a crumbling building Mama called a flophouse, and then back to the rooming house after John Dee came along.

Now there were no bedbugs, no drunken women in sweat-soiled corsets shouting on the stairs, no fires in the middle of the night to drive us out onto the street shivering in our petticoats. Worse than the dirty rooms where we lived were the men and the way they watched us. I could feel every time their eyes followed us down the stairs. They were following the changes in us, looking out for signs that we were becoming grown up. Maybe that's what kept Olive making baby talk until she was six or seven, and kept me in extra sweaters and blouses that buttoned up to my chin. All of that worry had fallen away when the Contraption rattled off into the night without us, replaced by a dull throb between my ribs, a kind of bruise I would have to live with.

Olive slumbered beside me. The only window was high up near the rafters and afforded no glimpse of moonlight. All I could see were the swaying trunks of fir trees, like giants sleepwalking in place.

On the first day at Eve Alice's we were allowed to explore. I was surprised by the amount of time it took to circle the house outside. We had to step carefully through the bracken and duck under an arch of vine maple that formed a green tunnel around the side of the house. Skipping through that bright passage became Olive's favorite thing to do.

There was a screened-in back porch, built to cover and protect a freshwater well with a crank and a bucket on a rope. There was also a hand pump and a tin cup, for drinking water.

Set a good ways back into the woods, the outhouse listed against a fir tree, walls mildewed by decades of rain and snow. It was plain and nothing luxurious, but Olive and I were used to sharing a first floor bath with three or four families. This was our very own outhouse.

Fifty feet or so from the back porch a post-and-wire fence sheltered a harem of busy hens watched over by a jocular red rooster. When Olive asked the rooster's name Eve Alice chuckled and said:

"Don't name what you might eat one day."

After a breakfast of biscuits and bitter coffee the three of us set off on a path that ran from the back of the house down to a ravine. A stream coursed from cool shade to bright patches where occasional sun broke the canopy. On the opposite ridge stood a few abandoned outhouses and sheds.

The stream flashed with lampreys. Eve Alice said it was spawning season. She promised to teach us how to hunt larger fish using a sharpened stick. Olive wrinkled her nose at the idea. She had never cared for fish up to that point and after she'd seen her first lamprey, its funnel mouth full of ring after ring of wicked little teeth, she said she might never go near the water again. She hated lampreys, she said, and then she couldn't stop telling us why.

"That's a monster," she said. "That's a monster from the sea... When it gets home it's going to grow as big as a ship... At night it comes up out of the ocean and drags the ships down, and eats everybody... That's a monster from Hell... That fish can suck your blood... Nobody knows how many teeth it has, maybe twenty-five or a hundred..."

We hiked alongside the stream for almost a mile and then followed a natural path uphill formed by crisscrossing terraces of grassy earth. We had to keep our eyes on the path for safe footing. When we emerged on level ground again we were standing at the outer edge of a large garden thick with wild shrubs, roses, ginger, and foxglove. Beyond this untended garden stood a large clapboard house. It had been whitewashed and seemed as clean and well cared for as the yard surrounding it was rough and neglected.

"Is this a castle?" Olive asked.

I told Eve Alice:

"We lived in a rooming house in Eugene. We only had two rooms. Livvy thinks a three-story house is where rich people live."

"Do not," said Olive. "I do not."

When we moved on and headed back down the crisscrossing path, Olive was still staring at the grand house. I had to come back and take little sister by the hand to lead her away.

That night we ate fried chicken and string beans. At first Olive made a face when she was offered the plate of chicken, but a growling stomach won out. Once we began to eat we couldn't stop, and it was as tender and delicious as any meal I'd ever tasted.

Eve Alice had a big appetite. She ate with gusto. She drank a bit of coffee with every meal, and cooled it by pouring a thimbleful from her cup into her saucer and then tipping the saucer up to sip it.

Olive insisted on calling Eve Alice 'Granny.' After the first few times no one objected and soon it seemed natural. I knew this was my sister's way of making herself at home.

"Granny," said Olive out of the blue that night. "Are you a Kanaka?"

Eve Alice chuckled and pushed her plate to one side. She leaned forward and rested her elbows on the table.

"Where did you hear that word, little plum?"

"John Dee said the river's full of Kanakas, and they'll come to get us if we don't watch out. Then he said you were a Kanaka."

"This man," said Eve Alice. "He's with your mama?"

We nodded yes.

"But he's not too smart, is he?"

This made me laugh in spite of myself. It felt good to laugh at John Dee without having to look around and make sure he wasn't listening.

"Your mama Claudine's a pretty one. That brings bad luck, sometimes. Pretty ones have to be careful. This man sounds like the boys she used to run with. Not good enough to keep up with her, but she doesn't know it. Don't trust a man who wears foolishness like it's a badge of honor, always talking, telling people the right way to say that and the best way to do this."

"That's John Dee all right," I told her.

"Count on most of what he says to be wrong."

"So, Granny," Olive said. "What's a Kanaka?"

"Kanaka Maoli is Hawaiian. It means 'the people.' Kanaka is a person. Back in the 1820s a trading company followed the Lewis and Clark route, and built the fort over at Vancouver. Workers came from all over. Some came all the way from the Hawaiian Islands. Sawyers cut the timber for shops and houses. Blacksmiths made nails and farm tools and traps the fur traders used."

"Were the fur traders Kanaka?"

"No. English and French Canadian. Then some rich Americans came over from New York to see what all the fuss was about. They found the river and they found things they wanted all along the river. Big men! Big business!"

Eve Alice laughed.

Mama had never talked about this place, not once. We were curious.

"Are we French Canadian, too?" I asked.

"No," Olive blurted out. "We're Injuns, right, Granny?"

That made me blush. Livvy could be childish, the way she repeated what John Dee said. But Eve Alice told her:

"Cowlitz, little plum. Some Cowlitz, some French Canadian, and some English. We get the name Dodd from the English part."

"Dodd?" I asked, because I'd never heard the name before.

"That's right, girl, what did you think your name was?"

"Mama said we came from the... the mountie..." Olive stopped. Struggling to remember the words made her wrinkle her forehead.

"*Mont des Morts*," I said.

Now Eve Alice laughed hard, a gusty sound that bounced off the walls of the kitchen and kept rolling around. After a moment she wiped her eyes with the back of her hand. Across the kitchen our reflection shone on the window against the black night outside.

"Your mama liked that name. She thought it sounded fancy. *Mont des Morts*! That's what the French Canadians called it," she explained.

"What is it?"

"Big black rock, upstream facing the river. Didn't you see it on your way here?"

"Delphie fell asleep," said Olive. "But I saw the rock."

"You didn't," I said.

"I did!"

"Why didn't you mention it before?"

"I don't have to tell you everything," Olive said. "Granny, it was coal black and shaped like a tombstone."

"That's it. Mount Coffin," said Eve Alice. "The sand and gravel company owns it now. Bought it from a rich family. You'll hear the blasting on some days. Barges carry the rocks away."

"To where?" Olive asked.

"Oh, all over. People pay good money for different sizes, for road fill, buildings, dams, what have you."

"But what was *Mont des... Mont des...*?"

"*Mont des Morts*," I said.

"What was it before, Granny?" Olive asked.

"First it was volcanic rock. It cooled off and sat for a long, long time, still and quiet, minding the riverbank until humans came to fish and then to live here. A lot more time went by, and gradually the rock became a solemn place to local people," Eve Alice said. "When I say local, I mean the families that lived along the river for thousands of years.

"And for a while after the Europeans came, the rock was still sacred. There were so many Chinook families here, and they were strong. Nobody from outside knew what the natives on the river might do. Back then the white Europeans bowed their heads when they sailed past the rock.

"Nobody injured the white men who went exploring on the rock, if they didn't break anything or steal souvenirs. Nevertheless, they got a friendly escort back to their ship after every visit."

"Goodbye, white men!" Olive said.

"That's right," said Eve Alice. "Europeans minded their own business when they saw warriors and weapons up and down the coast.

"One day, the world changed," Eve Alice continued. "The sun was bright on the shore. The water was cold and the current ran deep. In the river the fish were biting. Everything was just as it had been for as long as anyone could remember. Except on that day the children who went swimming in the river got sick and died. Pretty soon, almost everybody got sick. So many people died in some families, animals came to pick their bones because there was nobody to watch over them.

"After that, when visitors came to admire the rock, they took what they wanted. Men came to steal relics. There was no one strong enough to make them stop. Pretty soon the new laws called the land a frontier and gave anybody who moved here a piece of it to keep. So here they came by the boatload, by the cartload, on trains, in wagons.

"A family bought the rock. They built a house and a long picket fence. Their children ran up and down and all over. Big family. There were picnics and weddings and babies and more houses. Parties and dancing in the moonlight!

"Then came the flood. Some of the old folks said the river was sick of the new people and was tossing them out. But the new people wouldn't go until they were ready. By that time only the crows still met on Mount Coffin in the moonlight. Now the rock's only good for sand and gravel."

"But Granny," said Olive. "Why did the first white men bow their heads when they sailed past the rock?"

"Because it was covered with canoes, hundreds and hundreds of canoes. Inside were the bones of loved ones and precious things that belonged to them. That's how Chinook buried their dead, for as far back as anybody remembered. They buried their dead here. That's the place where we come from. That's where we are now. This area, all around you, the houses and roads, the canneries and timber companies, it's all grown up around that rock: Mount Coffin. *Mont des Morts.* The rock of the dead."

Before she put out the lantern that night, while we lay under the pile of quilts with only our heads sticking out, Eve Alice put her hand on my forehead and mumbled words I couldn't understand. She did the same with Olive. Then she placed around my neck a small leather pouch on a string, like the one she wore, and another around Olive's neck.

"What is it?" Olive asked.

"Good luck," said Eve Alice. "Nothing bad. It's a charm, a keepsake. Never take it off, and you'll stay safe."

"Safe from bears?" Asked Olive.

"Yes," said Eve Alice.

"And wolves?" I asked.

"Yes."

"What about spirits?" I asked.

Eve Alice studied our faces and said:

"Only spirits that were never buried, and never honored, have a complaint against us. As long as you wear this, they won't see you. Keep this magic, there's nothing bad about it. Keep this and don't be afraid."

Now we were curious, so we struggled out from under the quilts and opened the pouches. Olive squinted at hers. It looked like a crooked twig shaved to a sharp point.

"Dried witch finger," said Eve Alice.

Olive's eyes widened. "Not a real finger," she whispered.

"What good would a fake finger be?" Eve Alice said with a smile. Then she told us: "Nothing but cedar. Looks real, though."

I didn't know what to say. My gift wasn't a witch finger, real or fake. I was holding in my hand something I hoped wasn't genuine, although I didn't see how it could have been made, or why. Tiny enough to fit a child's face, it was a jawbone with the teeth intact.

I dreamed that the river flooded and washed the house away. Down into the waves all of our neighbors and the animals of the forest were pulled shrieking and struggling, their eyes staring, crazed. People sank in the mud. Cart horses were rushed along, beating their hooves against the waves, carried west with the current.

The river spread over the land all the way to the coast and knocked down houses in its path. The men and women sank like stones. On and on the waters spewed dying animals and the corpses of children, past the *Peter Iredale*, past the graveyard of all the ships that had wrecked along the shore, all the way west to the mighty mouth of the Columbia. There the river opened up and crashed against the ocean, dragging everyone, every ship and canoe and the broken bits of house frames down, down, rolling deep until the current released them and they drifted slow and lost to the bottom of the sea.

Our chores were easy enough to learn. Soon Olive and I found that we preferred certain tasks to other ones and we divided the work accordingly. We didn't mind. The life we had led up to that point seemed dull and useless by comparison. Working made a good change from sitting on the steps of the boarding house in Eugene playing marbles with boys who tried to cheat, and keeping count of the ladies we saw with exotic feathers attached to their hats.

Olive's favorite chore by far was churning butter. We traded eggs for milk from a neighbor's farm up the road. Eve Alice prepared the cream. Then Olive poured the cream into the churn and sat on a stool in the yard pumping the plunger for almost an hour. I didn't like the raw labor involved in churning. I hated to do the same thing for such a long time. I left it to Olive, to clean and snap the string beans too.

I learned from my grandmother the art of fishing with a dip net. Sometimes I brought home smelt, or the hideous but tasty lamprey, and sometimes I caught crawdads using a woven cedar trap.

I would follow Eve Alice on those occasions when she stepped into the chicken pen. I watched her closely, but I never got as good or as quick as she was at killing them. She said the trick was to never make a fuss, to accept what you had to do and then go about your business without scaring the animals. A scared chicken never tasted good, she said.

First she would open the gate and walk inside, scattering a little feed this way and that while she walked. The chickens would come around and cluck and peck at the ground, and she would make a little clucking noise too. She would choose the one she wanted and make her way toward it, taking her time, not changing her pace at all. Once she sidled up next to it she would go on with her little cluck-cluck noise, and with one hand she would dip down in a move that looked like a half curtsy. She would reach with her thumb pointed down and snatch that chicken by the neck, yank it up towards her and flip her wrist with a hard, solid snap. That was all it took. Her hands were strong from years of practice. The chicken might give a lurch or just fall in her arms, but it was dead before it knew it was dying. All the other chickens would fan out to the edges of the pen and let out a squawk or two, but in half a minute they would quiet down and start pecking at the ground again. This made me think chickens must be stupid. Eve Alice said they weren't stupid, only forgetful. I don't know. They never acted like they noticed their former friend hanging limp and dead from her hand as she left the pen.

Eve Alice told us we would both pick berries with her later on, in the summer. She explained how to look for wild strawberries and the juicy blackberries she would make into preserves we could sell and store for the winter. She grew string beans and lettuce and then bartered for what she needed. She laughed when Olive came back from foraging one day proudly offering a fistful of yellow flowers with glossy leaves shaped like a corn husk.

"Little plum," she said. "Can't you smell that?"

I caught a whiff and it turned my stomach. I had to look away and cough.

"What is it?" I asked.

"Skunk cabbage," said Eve Alice. "Pretty as can be when it pops up in the springtime. But don't pull it up and don't eat it."

"Why can't we eat it?" Olive asked. Trying to salvage what she had found on her own.

"It stinks!" I told her. "Now you stink, too."

"It burns your tongue," Eve Alice explained. "Only use it to wrap salmon, or line a basket. Or leave it where you find it and just look. If you get too close, it wears out its welcome."

Our grandmother's house had only three rooms aside

from the back porch. We washed our clothes on the porch. That was where the washboard and mangle were. If it was rainy on a laundry day, and it often was, we would hang the laundry to dry on the porch instead of in the yard.

Indoors we had our room upstairs and the downstairs main floor was divided in two. On one side was the kitchen with a pantry for canned food and preserves, and on the other side was Eve Alice's room. She kept her jars and powders and potions on small tables behind a painted screen. There were candles, black and green and red ones. A porcelain tray held a collection of threads and needles and scraps of fabric. The perfumes ranged from citrus to musk. The oils had various purposes, from soothing to conjuring. I didn't know the purpose for the smaller jars filled with hair and fingernail clippings. I soon learned that they came from the believers.

Eve Alice taught me and soon I was able to help prepare a few little remedies. We also traded fruit and vegetables with neighbors.

We seldom had to go into town. Many of the things we needed came by way of Sunday visitors. These were people who knew my grandmother or knew of her. They did not come to trade cream for eggs. Not on Sunday. They might roll up to the yard driving a Marmon, or a team of horses.

Eve Alice never invited or scheduled anyone. Somehow they arrived in graceful order, and allowed time to exchange a few words. They went away with what they needed: a strand of beads, a jar of oil, a candle and an incantation, a batch of tea, or nothing. The ones who left empty-handed were the believers. They handed over the nail clippings and hair strands, wrapped in hankies or transported in delicate purses. Eve Alice placed these items in glass jars until she was ready to use them.

The first time Olive and I delivered a batch of violet tea to the grand house with the garden, Eve Alice walked with us. She wasn't sure I could carry the clay jug by myself, but I've always been strong. Mama used to tell people her daughters were hearty and could live anywhere. By that she meant to explain how my first crib was a dresser drawer, and the only bedroom Olive and I ever had in Eugene was a cupboard.

"My girls can make themselves at home in a castle or a tent!" Mama once told a landlady who warned her that the room we rented was too small for children.

"This is much more on the tent side," the landlady said. She grinned a row of ragged teeth.

"We won't be here long," Mama assured the woman. "We're in town for the circus."

"Oh," said the landlady, brightening. "You're all in the circus?"

Mama fumed over that.

"I mean we're in town to see the circus!"

Too late, though, because the woman with rickety teeth told all the other residents we were circus folk. Mama hated that, but she couldn't live it down. Even after we moved to a rooming house on the other side of Eugene, if we ran into our old landlady she would remark on how hard it must be to keep in training for the circus.

Once we settled in with Eve Alice I never talked about those old times again. I didn't like the way grownups would look at me when they knew how poor we had been, or that my mother left us. Her absence confused me more as time went on, more than the first night, because we didn't hear from her after that. We expected a letter to say she was all right but week after week brought us no news.

The violets were Johnny-jump-ups. Eve Alice pulled off the leaves and we ate those as cooked greens. We picked the flowers on an overcast day, or in the morning before the sun broke through. Eve Alice explained that we didn't want the flowers to dry out. We were after the oil in the petals.

We washed off the dirt carefully because the flowers were delicate. Then we tied them in bunches and hung them upside down in the kitchen behind a screen, where there wasn't much light. Since the stove was nearby this was the warmest spot in the house. After a couple of weeks we took them down, pinched off the petals, and placed them in glass jars and sealed them up. Two teaspoons of dried violets to one cup of boiling water produced a strong brew, delicious to taste, with a soothing effect on the nerves. Eve Alice warned us to drink small amounts because it could also serve as a laxative.

We followed the path down into the ravine and alongside the stream. I asked why we couldn't carry the tea across on level ground to the grand house. Eve Alice said the forest between the two houses was still wild, dense, and muddy. Walking there wasn't practical. We might sink into the mud and never be found. Best to keep to the route she had been using for as long as she could remember, she told us. It was a path used by her mother and grandmother long before the grand house was built. Then she told us it wasn't a grand house but a "sanitarium," where young ladies of means came to take "the cure."

"What's the cure?" Olive asked.

"Your sister's carrying part of the cure in that jug," Eve Alice said. "We brew different kinds of tea and sometimes we make broth. Doctor Graham pays by the batch."

"Doctor Graham?"

"She's got a system the ladies use to get their health back. They rest and eat good food and drink tea."

"A lady doctor?" Livvy found this very funny.

"Women can be doctors," I told her. "What's wrong with the young ladies at the sanitarium?"

Eve Alice considered the question for a minute. Then she said:

"Likely there's nothing wrong that a walk and a strong cup of tea wouldn't fix."

"Why do they come to the doctor?" I asked.

"These are ladies from rich families. All their lives they've been told to sit down and be quiet," she said. "They've gotten it into their heads that they ought to enjoy being quiet. If they don't like it, if they want to get up and run, or break something, they think it's unnatural. They think they're sick in the heart, or in the lungs. They get headaches. They cry."

"But how do they know about Doctor Graham?" I said.

"Oh, she wrote a book," Eve Alice explained. "Women pass it around, and tell each other Doctor Graham's got a cure for any ailment. People tell their friends. The way our Sunday visitors tell other people. Word gets around, even when nobody says anything."

"But it's your tea, Granny," said Olive. "You should be famous. You're the one that makes the cure."

"Oh no," said Eve Alice. "This is just one remedy the ladies drink, to make them feel calm. I don't know all the things the doctor tells them to do. Probably they eat rich food and take long walks and go to bed early."

"Where do they go?" I asked.

"Go?"

"They're not walking by the stream, or we would see them," I said. "If they can't walk in the woods, where do they go?"

"Probably up the road in front of the sanitarium. Maybe they all walk into town together."

"I think you should be famous, Granny," Olive said again.

"Little plum, making remedies and being famous don't go together. Plenty of women could tell you that. What we do here is just for our friends and our Sunday visitors, and Doctor Graham. She doesn't tell anyone what we do, and we don't talk about the sanitarium to outsiders. Understand?"

We nodded gravely. I think we felt privileged to be included in these grown-up matters. I took my duties to heart.

That first trip was slow going up the crisscrossing terraces. Finally we reached the back garden of the sanitarium. We crossed the garden on the trail of smooth stones and came to a portico with a brass bell.

Eve Alice rang the bell and we waited. It seemed like several minutes before the door opened and a slim middle-aged woman stepped onto the landing. She was spotless in her uniform, a starched apron over a dark dress with a white kerchief covering her hair. Her face was slender, with eyes like a bird's and thin lips that barely moved when she spoke.

"The doctor says to thank you for your trouble," she said. She looked us over. "So you have your little helpers," she told Eve Alice.

"They're hard workers," my grandmother said with a smile.

"I'm Nurse Allen," the woman told Olive and me. "I'll only be a minute."

She took the jug from my hands. Then she closed the door. Eve Alice waited. Olive and I didn't move until the woman came back and handed me the empty jug. She gave Eve Alice some coins.

This time I noticed a second door, every bit as sturdy as the one with the brass bell, but set back several feet inside the portico. When Nurse Allen came to speak with us she closed that inner door behind her before she opened the outer door.

"The doctor asks if you would be kind enough to bring two batches next time," she said.

"Two?" Eve Alice asked.

"We have two new guests arriving soon," the woman said. "We expect a full house by next week."

Eve Alice said nothing. As we followed her back down the stone walkway through the garden, I heard the woman click the bolt into place. All the way home I wondered what the young ladies were so afraid of. Bears? Wolves? Men like John Dee who might lure them away from the cure and make them dance with him in the moonlight? That would be the most terrible danger, I thought. I was still very young and nothing was clear to me yet.

For two months I carried tea and broth to the sanitarium. Olive made the trip with me, a few times a week, and when double batches were needed Eve Alice came along.

One day we spotted a bear on the ridge overlooking the stream. Olive and I froze in our tracks. The bear swung his big brown head and spittle flew from his jaws. Then we saw the bees swarming around his head. He batted at them, grumbled, then gave up his honey prize and went trundling up toward the timberline. Through all of this, he paid no attention to us.

The only creatures that took note when we were outdoors were the crows. There were days when they showed slight interest, checking our presence and then darting off into the trees. On blasting days, however, when we felt the ground rumble under our feet, the crows sometimes followed us all the way to the sanitarium. Their habit was to shadow us at a short distance. They took turns harrumphing into the air, flapping two or three times and landing again behind us.

In the summer we picked wild strawberries. On some days our neighbors Mandy Swann and her son Gilbert joined us. Mandy was as wide as she was tall. She called both of us girls "pet" and brought us bits of chocolate and nickels to keep. She taught Olive needlework and told us stories. She also made remedies, but she didn't have Sunday visitors. Mandy's work was more secret than our grandmother's.

Gilbert was a slow child, but the sweetest boy I ever met. He loved music and watching birds. One time he wove a hat for Livvy to wear in the sun. He decorated it with a couple of crow feathers he had found.

"Wear this so only the crows see you," he explained.

"They might peck my eyes out," said Olive.

"No," said Gilbert. "They recognize you."

He grinned and the constellation of freckles on his face lit up. His blue-green eyes sparkled.

The five of us had a fine time picking strawberries and

putting up jam for the faraway winter. Olive and I learned to make preserves and tea, but not for the sanitarium. Nurse Allen said the doctor had no use for strawberry because it might "counteract the regimen." She asked if Eve Alice could make a dandelion brew or if she cultivated devil's club.

"No, but I've put away more jars of dried violets," Eve Alice said.

Nurse Allen said the violet tea would be fine, or chicory, if we had any. Then she asked about juniper berries and Eve Alice told her those grew in a dry climate, further east.

Olive and I knew very well that we had devil's club at home. One time when Olive had upset stomach I made her chew on devil's club bark until she vomited. Eve Alice said next time a cup of mint tea would be better, and not to experiment on Livvy without permission. Devil's club was nothing to play around with, even if we had plenty of it. So when Nurse Allen asked what we could offer, Olive and I followed our grandmother's lead and said nothing.

That summer Mandy and Gilbert spent as much time at our house as theirs. We liked to cook supper outdoors. Mandy and Eve Alice prepared smoked salmon and corn. Dessert was a batch of Mandy's blackberry ice cream. Olive and Gilbert and I would play cards and listen to the women talk about people they knew and days gone by.

One night after the sun went down we sat on the grass and watched the sky for shooting stars. The woods grew black around us. In the dark beyond our fire we could hear the stream and the rustling of wings. At the sound of a sharp caw, Olive reached for her crow hat and placed it on her head.

Mandy offered to tell us a tale from her mother's family.

"When Mommy was a little girl everybody for miles around knew this story by heart. So many people have moved away since then, and common knowledge isn't common anymore."

We gathered around. The women sipped strawberry

wine while Mandy told us the story:

"After the Bostons— excuse me, I mean the white men— realized the fever killed natives and didn't kill whites, all hell broke loose. Boats came every week, docking at Mount Coffin. Most of the children had died by then. They were sick for a short time but they were wretched. Their poor little bodies ached with pain we can't even imagine. Their mothers watched them die. They couldn't do a thing about it."

In the forest was a rustling noise. I squinted into the dark but I couldn't pinpoint the source of the restless movement.

"Eventually, most of the grownups died too. Those who didn't die were weak, and in pain. Among the women a few, just a few, recovered from the fever. These women tried to tend to the weaker ones, the old people and the babies, but none of their remedies or charms or prayers made any difference. Their friends and parents and children all passed over. Everyone they loved passed over.

"Some of the white explorers offered what medicine they had, and mourned the death of people they had come to respect. Other men saw an opportunity.

"Charles Dabney was one of those men. In the past he had sailed to Mount Coffin three times, with no success. Every time he landed, men had been standing guard. Dabney's raiders had been outnumbered and afraid.

"Although the local families had made it clear, back then, that they wouldn't tolerate a disturbance of the dead, they were generous in their habits. They invited the visitors to rest and enjoy a meal before they left. Sometimes their invitations were accepted and sometimes not. Their hospitality made it clear that there were no hard feelings, only a line drawn between what was allowed and not allowed. On each one of Dabney's expeditions the natives had treated their disappointed guests to a meal of sturgeon, roots, berries, wapato, and salmon."

A dark flutter caught my eye. I stared into the woods,

into the shadows.

"Now the warriors were gone. The elders were gone. Only a few of the women were alive, and they witnessed the worst things men can do.

"In the middle of the night Dabney led his fourth and final expedition up Mount Coffin. He set his men loose to scavenge for anything valuable they could get their hands on. They broke into burial canoes and looted them. They stole glass beads, animal skins, tools, and weapons. All of these belonged to the dead.

"Worse than that, Dabney was under contract to a collector who wanted to catalog every tribe he could find. He paid a high price for skulls he could put on display."

In the trees a tiny pair of eyes appeared. Then another.

"The women could only shake their heads and weep while the men stripped the dead of belongings, even their bones. After the men helped themselves to what they wanted, including skulls of the dead, they turned to the women, expecting food. And now that they could demand what they pleased, they expected other forms of hospitality."

Olive looked up at Mandy and said, "Hospitality?"

Dozens of pairs of eyes sparkled in the trees. The crows were perfectly silent and still.

"These men thought the world owed them anything they wanted. The women obliged, smiling, gentle as could be, and the men thought their smiling faces showed how simple they were.

"'See how the savages give way underfoot,' Dabney told his men. 'This is their fate. They accept it, as children accept that their parents are stronger, better in mind and spirit.'

"Three of the women gave themselves to him that night. The others prepared a feast. All of the men gorged themselves on sturgeon and mussels and clams, and on wine they had brought from their ship. The women indulged them in every way."

As high as I could see in the surrounding fir trees, crows dotted the branches. They made no sound now.

"By midnight the men were drunk and shouting that they felt no pain for the dead, no pain for anything!"

"Them savages," whispered Gilbert.

Olive nodded and said:

"Monsters."

Mandy nodded. She took a sip of wine.

"By morning," she said. "Every man in Dabney's party lay dead on the shore."

"How?" Olive asked.

"Some lucky ones had passed quickly from the poison, and some died in a bad way. Dabney bled out, watching the women cut his entrails loose with a knife while he was lying there, paralyzed on the sand."

Suddenly Mandy and Eve Alice laughed. Because his mother was laughing, Gilbert laughed too.

Livvy watched the women with her round, soft eyes and then turned to me, but I didn't know what to say. I liked the story, and I liked the idea of Dabney screaming for his life in a pool of blood.

I looked up at the trees, but there was nothing. No crows, nothing.

"If those men had spent one month here," said Eve Alice. "They would have learned which shellfish were safe, and when. Every place, where red tide poisoned the mussels and clams, was marked with a sign. Everybody knew not to fish there for a certain number of seasons. They knew when and where it was safe to eat the fish. You have to know a place if you want to take what it has to offer."

"Wouldn't have done those men any good, knowing," said Mandy. "The fish they ate wasn't bad."

"Oh, that's true," said Eve Alice.

Olive and I looked at each other.

"So, what killed Dabney's men?" I asked.

"Red algae," said Mandy.

"You said the fish wasn't bad."

"It wasn't the fish they ate, but what was used to season it."

"Now listen to this," Eve Alice said directly to me. Mandy continued:

"You take shellfish from red tide and boil it, throw the fish away, dry what's left and crush it into a powder. It's easy to store in a jar. Looks like any other seasoning. Any time you need it, add water and pour it in with a few spices. That's what the women did. That's how they showed their hospitality to Dabney. They added spice."

Eve Alice repeated the word.

"Spice."

From then on, whenever the two women were together, all one of them had to do was say the word 'spice' and they would nod or smile. Most of the time they were kindly old women, not a mean bone in their bodies. When they used the word 'spice' a magic line was drawn between them and the rest of the world. It was nothing I could explain, but I felt it as surely as a sudden drop in the temperature.

In one of my dreams the river cut through our house. It ran under the floorboards, down the hill, and formed the stream out back.

If someone died they didn't know it. They went on walking until their skin fell away. They left their skin on the ground, crawled through the vine maple around the side of our house, down the path, and slithered into the stream.

Olive and I were outside, bathing. The lampreys swam around us but when we reached out to catch them our hands moved through them and they grew bigger. They twitched in the water and hid their funnel mouths below the surface in the rotten weeds.

The phantoms crept in and out of the water trying to get clean but they had no skin. Every time they entered the stream, scarlet jets of blood shot through the water.

I woke with the taste of metal on my tongue.

Our summer weather varied. We might have two weeks of sunny days and suddenly the rain would return, cold as early spring. On one of these unseasonable days it just so happened that I had to walk to the sanitarium by myself.

Olive lay in bed with a slightly elevated temperature, probably nothing but the change in barometric pressure, but you could never be sure. Eve Alice decided to stay home and keep an eye on her.

The mist had risen from the forest floor. A thin fog drifted across the stream and gently distorted its natural shape, making it tricky to follow by sight. My view of the ridge opposite was intermittent. Then the ridge faded altogether. I was careful to stick close to the path I knew, my shoes clicking on the pebbled shore.

About two thirds of the way, as I passed a cluster of exposed roots jutting from the bluff on my side of the stream, I had a feeling that someone was watching me. I glanced around but didn't see any crows.

The woods and the ravine could be eerie at certain times of day. Once, early in the morning, Olive and I had seen a wolf drinking from the stream. It raised its head, gazed left and right with shocking gray-blue eyes, lowered its snout, and went on drinking. None of the animals we encountered ever showed an interest, and I never went anywhere without my leather pouch with the tiny jawbone inside. Olive had to be reminded.

"I'm not afraid of bears," she would say. Or, "That wolf didn't scare me."

"It's because of the witch finger," I told her.

"How do you know?"

"Livvy, animals aren't afraid of girls."

"Maybe they're afraid of me. I can roar."

"Don't be stupid," I said. "Keep this pouch around your neck, even when you sleep. If you don't, I'll tell on you."

"I'm not scared of wolves, or you," she whined.

"If you don't do as Eve Alice said, the lampreys will eat

you," I told her. That did the trick.

The morning I went alone to the sanitarium, there were no wolves or bears. I caught a glint of light from the water and turned, but no one was there.

I walked on. The sensation of being stalked grew with every step. I wanted to turn again, to assure myself that I was wrong, but I couldn't make myself look.

People often told me I was a sensible girl. Olive was pretty, they said, and I was sensible. I drew on all of my good sense to shut out the uneasiness, but the further along I walked, the stronger it grew. Where I was felt too far from home and too far from my destination, to run. Without meaning to, I found myself staring down at the good luck charm around my neck and wishing I knew a prayer or a chant I could repeat.

I couldn't run for fear of spilling the broth Eve Alice had prepared. I didn't see how I could tell her I just got scared and ran away. That would cost us the day's wages. So I said to myself, again and again, the words I recalled from an old book Mama had given us when we were little:

"Over the river and through the woods... Over the river and through the woods... Over the river and through the woods..."

I must have said this a hundred times, faster and faster as the fear rose up and I felt the cold mist sweep against my back. I huffed and puffed all the way up the crisscrossing terraces, stomping with every step to make sure of my footing, feeling against my chest the pouch with the charm inside, and clutching the jug with both hands. Up the final steps, out of breath, still chanting the words, I climbed until the garden was almost at eye level. With a final hop I was standing at the edge of the garden, and there I stopped dead.

Amid the drifting fog and the ruins of untended rose bushes a gray-white figure emerged. Its shroud clung to jutting bones, and tangled in a mass at the ankles. Stark feet stuck out below the shroud. The figure hung there for a second then started to rotate, so slowly I had time to feel the hairs rising on my arms. Once it faced me I could see its mouth hung open, silent, with long strands of spit on either side.

I dropped the clay jug, spilling all of its contents. The warm liquid hit the ground and steam rose from the spot.

I stood frozen, staring. The figure gave a little jerk of its head and seemed to notice me. It headed in my direction with one shoulder thrust forward and the shroud catching at its ankles with every step. Without a thought in my head I screamed.

At the sound of my scream the figure looked up with wild eyes and changed direction. Nurse Allen dashed from the back door into the garden and shouted something over her shoulder. Another nurse appeared, followed by a woman in a blue dress, and the three ran straight for the figure in the shroud. As I watched, the nurses and the woman I guessed to be Doctor Graham fanned out and surrounded the figure, which I could now see was only a woman, a real woman, with deadly pale skin.

The woman gave an animal shriek of panic. She clawed at her face and at the sheer gown clinging to her like a second skin. The other women moved in with their arms spread wide. They formed a circle and tightened like a noose around the screaming woman until she couldn't escape. Another nurse came running from the house with a blanket. The four of them wound it around and around the woman until she could no longer move. She was whimpering like an injured animal when the nurses lifted her into their arms and carried her into the house.

I felt the cold rushing against my back again. My teeth chattered. The woman in the blue dress, Doctor Graham, came creeping toward me, taking more and more careful steps as she approached the end of the garden. I wanted to back up but I knew the ground fell away behind me. Doctor Graham kept inching along, leaning forward until her face was next to mine. She glanced down at the spot where I'd dropped the clay jug.

"It's all right, girl," she said.

Her voice was flat and calm, as though the struggle with the woman had never taken place. She smelled like clean laundry and rubbing alcohol.

"Now, now," she coaxed. "Listen to me, girl. Don't be afraid. I won't tell your granny to punish you for ruining the medicine. We can do without our broth for once. It's all right."

She reached into the pocket of her dress, took out some coins, and held them out to me. When I didn't take them she placed them in the palm of my hand and closed it into a fist.

"Let's pretend you made the delivery as usual. We won't say a word about this, will we?"

I wasn't sure how to explain what had happened. The doctor was important enough to draw rich young ladies from all parts of the country to take her cure, and we relied on the doctor for a part of our income.

The woman I saw might have been insane. She might have been sick with fever. I only knew one thing for sure about the sanitarium and about Doctor Graham: They had the power to keep a woman against her will.

After supper, when Olive had been given a dose of remedy for her cold and had fallen asleep, I sat at the kitchen table with Eve Alice. I told her everything I had seen that morning.

When I was done my grandmother sat staring at her hands on the table. I thought my worst fear had come true. She didn't believe me. She thought I was a liar. She might even send me away for making up stories about her best customer.

Just when I couldn't stand the silence any more Eve Alice said:

"All right, Delphine. I'll talk with Mandy. We know what to do. You were smart to tell me right away. That's good. If you're afraid of anything, you tell me, and I'll take care of it."

I'd never felt such relief. That night I slept soundly and without dreaming.

A few days passed. Olive recovered and became her usual self, chattering and making up stories. Eve Alice made trips to the sanitarium alone during that time.

One evening I was setting my crawdad traps. I would place the traps soon after dark, in spots where I'd noticed a lot of grass or algae under the water. This was where they liked to hide. By morning I'd have a good supply and we would eat very well that day.

Olive was making fun of me, calling me 'Queen Crawdad,' and I was threatening her with no supper, when I noticed movement on the ridge, on our side of the stream. I might not have pinpointed the women in the dusk and shadows if I hadn't also heard the crunch of shovels in dirt.

"What's the matter?" Livvy asked. I shushed her.

I motioned for her to do as I did. We crouched and crept sideways to the edge of the woods. From there we could see the two nurses who had helped the doctor and Nurse Allen catch the woman in the garden. Now they wore dark dresses without their white aprons and kerchiefs, but I recognized them at once.

"They're nurses," I whispered to Olive and she asked:

"What are they doing?"

I was wondering the same thing. This was a good long walk upstream from the sanitarium.

We stayed hidden at the edge of the ridge and watched as they finished digging a hole between two large sword ferns. When they stopped digging one of them said:

"This ought to be enough."

"It doesn't look very deep," said the other one.

"I'm not staying out here all night. It's deep enough."

They picked up a bundle of cloth rags and tossed it down into the hole. Then they put in another and another.

When they had thrown in half a dozen bundles, one of them threw in a wide-brimmed hat with a ribbon attached.

"Oh, that's a shame," said the second nurse. "I don't have a hat for Sundays."

"Quiet," said the first one. "I'm not risking the gallows for a smart hat. You fool."

They turned the pile of dirt back into the hole and patted the surface with the shovels. Then they picked up leaves and scattered them over the spot.

When they were done they headed downstream toward the sanitarium. We saw them climb down from the ridge when they came to a ditch with a boulder in the middle. From there they continued on the path we had taken each time we carried tea or broth to the doctor. They must have known, as we did, that the rest of the forest wasn't safe.

Olive wanted to dig up the bundles. I think she had her eye on that hat. But I told her no and we had to go right home, because Eve Alice needed to know what we had seen.

Early the next morning I heard voices downstairs. Olive was still snoring away, so I went down to the kitchen. Mandy was sitting at the table with Eve Alice. They looked up when I entered the room. Mandy nodded and said:

"Hello, pet."

On the table between them were scraps of material, twine, needles and thread. There were jars full of oil, and a bowl full of copper-red powder. Mandy held a miniature rag doll and fussed with its blue dress.

I sat at the table. I couldn't take my eyes off the bright powder. The two women exchanged a glance and Mandy told me:

"If you want to stop someone, you need a likeness."

She held up the doll. Its dress matched the one I had seen Doctor Graham wearing.

"You've got to sew a message inside, with this."

She touched a finger to the rim of the bowl. She dipped her finger in the powder and tasted it.

"Cayenne," she said.

I exhaled at last.

"And you need one thing from the person you want to stop."

"What does stop mean?" I asked.

"Not kill," said Eve Alice. "She might come down with a fever. She might twist her ankle. It depends on what you do with the likeness once it's ready. If you bury it far away, she might get lost in the woods."

All of this seemed useless to me. And temporary.

"Do you have one thing that belongs to Doctor Graham?" I asked.

"No," said Eve Alice. "I've tried to get inside, tried every excuse. I caught a glimpse of a nurse's station inside. I'm guessing they take shifts all day and night."

"Tell her," said Mandy.

Eve Alice shook her head. Mandy told me:

"There might be a way to get in, but it's tricky. We can't do it. You and Olive..."

"No," said Eve Alice. "Not worth it."

The woman in the garden loomed in my mind. I saw her eyes searching for a way out. I saw the nurses surround her and trap her like an animal.

"Then go get the sheriff and let a man take care of it," said Mandy with a grin.

"Graham's got the sheriff wrapped around her pinky. She'll sweet talk him, and send him back here."

"You and I can't go to jail, Eva," said Mandy. "We've got these children, and they've got nobody else."

At the mention of jail Eve Alice looked me in the eye. I knew right then what we had to do.

"I'll sneak into the sanitarium and find Doctor Graham's room," I said. "I'll steal something that belongs to her."

Then I set my shoulders squarely, to let them know I wouldn't take no for an answer. I was a strong woman, too.

One thing we had noticed was that Nurse Allen never used a key. This was as damning as anything because it meant she didn't have to lock the patients inside. She must have known they were too sick or too weak to work the bolt. The woman I saw in the garden must have waited a long time for her chance at an unbolted door.

That time of year twilight came late. We waited until it was completely dark and cool, and so quiet we could hear the splash of fish all the way from the stream. We must have made a weird sight when the faint moonlight washed over us: Two old women and two little girls creeping along. We'd had the good sense to leave Gilbert at home because nobody ever knew when he might start talking up a storm. For this task we needed complete quiet.

When we reached the sanitarium we stationed Olive near the front door. I stayed at the back. Eve Alice took her place behind the shrubs that ran down the side of the garden, and Mandy hid in the shadows ready to run for help if it came to that. It was so dark by that time it's a wonder we didn't break an ankle, or worse.

During the day we used the brass bell but this sounded through the whole house. So I knocked on the back door. Then I jumped down from the portico, darted into the shadows, and hunched down on the ground.

One of the young women Olive and I had seen in the woods opened the door and took a look around. I guess she decided she was hearing things because she went right back inside and bolted the doors.

I heard a call that might have been a crow but was really Eve Alice. This was followed by the far off sound of Olive knocking at the front door. Soon we heard the nurse open the door, pause to check outside, and then close it.

She wasn't as bright or as diligent as Nurse Allen. It only took two rounds of this game for the young woman to lose her patience and leave both back doors ajar while she scurried down the hall to the front door, in a vain hope of catching the culprit in the act.

While she surveyed the side of the house and cussed under her breath about damn country people, I slipped right into the house.

First I spotted the nurse's station. There was an oak desk with a lamp and file cabinets. Past that a short wide hallway divided the main floor in half. On the left side were two doors. On the right there was a stairway with mahogany banisters. I followed my instinct and raced around to the stairs. A potted fern blocked my progress on the landing. I edged around it.

All of the windows upstairs were covered with heavy curtains. The air was stagnant with a nauseating combination of fuchsia and alcohol.

Up to this point I had been following Eve Alice's instructions but she wasn't sure of the layout of the place. I felt a wave of anger and impatience, a sure sign that I was out of my depth. I reminded myself that this was, partially, my plan. It would work or it would fail depending on how brave I was. I tried to think calmly.

If I kept somebody weak on medicine, I wouldn't worry much about her escape. So maybe the patients had rooms on the first and second floors.

If I wanted to sleep soundly I'd give myself a nice room upstairs. That's why I passed right by the rooms on the second floor and headed up to the third. It would be more private up there. The view would be the finest there.

Just as I cleared the third flight of stairs I heard the nurse closing the front door. I didn't know how much time I had before somebody woke up and caused a commotion. Luckily there was only one door at the top of the landing. I could hear the nurse downstairs, still cussing. I held my breath and pushed the door as gently as I could.

It was pitch dark at first. Then the room began to take shape before me.

Two beds with wrought iron frames were pushed up against the walls on either side of a narrow space. There was no other furniture, and no pictures. No chairs. I could barely see the outline of a window on the far wall. Unlike the ones downstairs, this window had no curtain. In fact it seemed to be painted over. If I had left right at that moment, I might have said the room was empty.

I stood in the middle of that close space and tried to catch my breath. The air reeked of accumulated sweat. Damp skin brushed against my arm. I jumped back, and landed on one of the beds. The sheets felt damp. A movement at my side told me I wasn't alone and before I could escape it took shape: A woman, raw and thin as a skeleton, lay close beside me. The way the skin hung from her cheekbones and arms, I would have thought she was dead if she hadn't moved her lips. Her mouth was dry and chapped and broken in places. No sound came from her throat except a dark whisper without words.

I sprang back to the middle of the room. In the opposite bed a woman reached out. She was searching, but I don't think she saw me. Like the first woman, she was too weak to sit up, so emaciated and sunken into the center of the bed she could barely move at all.

My heart was thumping. I could hear the blood coursing through my whole body. I had to get out. I backed up through the door and pulled it shut. I had to move. Nothing I could do or say was going to get me out of there alive except my own two feet.

I crept down the stairs. The sweat was coursing down my back and my armpits were soaked. I snuck out the front door, pulling it shut behind me.

We were silent women, silent girls tiptoeing through the night, until we reached the stream. Naturally, Olive broke first.

"What happened? What did you *see*?" She shrieked.

"The young ladies," I managed to say. "Two ladies."

"Were they sick?" Mandy asked.

"Did they talk to you?" Eve Alice asked.

"No, no," I fumbled for words.

"What did you see?" Olive demanded again.

"Starving!" I shouted. "They're starving to death in there. Those women are dying."

All night I prayed I would live long enough to forget those women, and forget that I left them there to save my own hide. But that's how the mind works. It forgets what you love and want to hold onto, and it makes a special, permanent place for all the things you wish you'd never seen.

My heart was still racing when we got home. Eve Alice made me drink chamomile with a tincture added, and finally I fell asleep.

Next day I started shivering all over. Eve Alice made me stay in bed. I slept for two days, waking up long enough to sip the hot lemon tea my sister and grandmother fed me with a spoon, and then falling back into a fever sleep. All that time I dreamed.

The rains came. The stream overflowed, turned into a river, and washed up over the ridge. The waters rose to our back porch with twigs and branches floating on the surface.

I opened the screen door. I saw the river flowing right beneath my feet, filled with animal skins and human bodies. The corpses were sewn into dirty white shrouds that tore away under the battering rain. Beneath the shrouds someone had sewn their limbs to their torsos, and had sewn their eyes and mouths shut. When the shrouds tore away the corpses slid out, pale and slippery, into the river.

I tried to push the bodies away, to keep them from floating into the house, but there were so many and I hated to touch them. When my hand touched their skin they felt slick. I could see up close that their skin had turned gray and they were bloated, ready to burst open. I ran upstairs, but no one else was home and I knew the waters would rise until they drowned me.

After many days the rain stopped. For weeks and

weeks I slept in a cot in the yard drinking lemon tea. When I finally woke I was upstairs in bed. Olive was gone. Her footprints led down to the main floor, outside and away from the house. I followed them to the ravine.

Fog rolled in and covered the stream. I heard splashing, a body rolling over and over in the water. I called out:

"Livvy!"

The splashing stopped. I crept forward, searching. I spied the dark body of a lamprey sliding through the stream. It kept emerging from the water and disappearing again.

In the fog I could barely make out the shape of my sister's gown clinging to her body. She lay face down, floating in the reeds with her arms splayed.

Shivering in my gown, I cried out for my sister and I stepped forward until my bare feet found the icy water. It rushed in around my ankles and tugged at my feet. I stood with my feet sinking in sand and stones.

"Livvy!" I shouted.

Now I was unable to see through the fog. I heard splashing again, much closer. I was overcome by the sense of someone watching me, someone I couldn't see no matter how hard I tried.

Out of the fog came shovel-nosed canoes, dozens of them. I stood in the middle of a vast lake only a few feet deep. The canoes came gliding toward me on all sides, guided by warriors I could barely see. As they drew closer I realized that the skin on their faces had been cut off. The skull shone through on some. On others the muscles and eye sockets remained.

I tried to scream. Only the sound of water rose up, the waves spattering against my gown. As they floated past me on all sides, the canoes cut my body. Each wound opened and splayed in the icy lake, and I felt my lungs and kidneys being torn from underneath.

I didn't know what day it was when I woke up. Eve Alice gave me a sponge bath on the back porch. Then she bundled me up, although it looked like a warm summer day outside. I sat in a large chair in the kitchen and sipped tea. Light skittered and danced across the floor from a small window at the side of the house. Gradually I dozed off again.

I heard knocking at the front door. This was unusual because our neighbors were in the habit of opening the door and calling hello, then walking right in. I waited, thinking Eve Alice would answer. Then the knocking came again.

As I opened the door a man with ginger hair pulled a wide-brimmed straw hat from his head and nodded.

"Can I help you?" I asked.

"Thank you kindly," he said. "I would be grateful."

He had an accent I had never heard before, with a lilt so that he seemed to be asking a question. He wore a vest with pockets over a loose fitting shirt and trousers. A watch chain stretched across the vest. In one hand he held his straw hat and in the other he held a compass.

He wasn't a neighbor. In my addled condition I thought: *This is another dream. I'm only thinking of this, and doing these things in my sleep.*

"Well," I said after a moment. "How can I help you?"

"My need is easily met, gracious lady," he said, and it occurred to me that maybe he was mocking me. "This morning I have spent hours surveying the riverbank."

"Surveying?"

"Yes ma'am."

"Do you work for the gravel company?" I asked.

"My patron is not Hudson's Bay, if that is what you ask. But I have letters of recommendation."

"For what?" I asked.

"I beg your pardon," he said with a blush. "I've come to offer condolences."

"Why?"

"Oh, I see," he said. "You're a child. Forgive me. May I request a drink of water?"

Even if this was a dream, it seemed strange to me that a workingman would go off for the day without any water. Also, the company he named sounded familiar, although I couldn't place it. This, I imagined, was proof that I was dreaming. Otherwise how could I have such a strong sense of knowing what I didn't know?

"Wait here," I told him. "I'll fetch you a cup from the well."

"Thank you," he said.

On the back porch I used the hand pump to fill a tin cup with water, and I was happy to find that my strength was coming back. Once I had a good amount of cold water to offer I returned to the front door.

I wasn't all that surprised not to see the man when I opened the door. I thought maybe he had stepped away from the house out of politeness. But I didn't find him in the yard, or around the side of the house, or along the edge of the woods. Finally I walked out to the road and scanned as far as I could see. There was Mandy's house, fringed by fir trees, and the spot way off where the dirt road climbed up and disappeared to the west. But the man with the straw hat and ginger hair was nowhere to be seen.

When I woke it was almost noon. Olive was holding my hand, and Eve Alice was gone.

"Granny says to rest all day," Olive said.

"Is she going to get the sheriff?" I asked.

"She didn't say. Mandy cooked a batch of soup and they went out. Said they'd be back soon and not to follow. Gilbert's picking blackberries so you can have a pie when you get well."

"Did you say they made soup?"

"Chowder I guess. With clams and corn and potatoes. She said it was a winter soup, but some people are greedy and like to eat a hearty meal in the summertime."

"What did she mean? What else did they say?"

"I don't know," Olive said. "Let me pour you a cup of tea, sister."

Eve Alice returned alone within the hour. She washed up and cleaned the house. She put the herb garden and her collection of potions in good order. She burned sage.

She put her hand on my forehead and spoke words I didn't understand, the way she had the night she gave me the leather pouch I had worn every day since. She stroked my hands and called me her daughter, and said it would all be well. We had done a good thing and it would all be well.

Mandy brought us all of the gossip as she heard it. We followed the story as it took shape over the weeks and months.

First came news that the milkman couldn't rouse Nurse Allen or the doctor for his weekly payment. He had tried the back door but no one answered. Finally he let the sheriff know something was wrong.

They found the bodies of three nurses and Doctor Graham in various rooms of the house. No one could understand what drove the doctor to poison her staff and herself, until the whole house was opened up. Then it was agreed by most people that a woman who could do what she had done to her patients was capable of almost anything.

It was a measure of how respectable and sly and prosperous Doctor Graham was, that no one had ever questioned what she was up to. People said she had flattered anyone who needed to be flattered, and paid anyone who needed cash. She had written a book that made her sound like an expert on good health and vitality. She had spoken softly and accepted money and gifts from well-to-do ladies. It turned out that most of them had even changed their wills or left bequests to the sanitarium. Most likely these transactions took place while they were in the throes of their first few weeks of starvation, flush with energy and strange ideas.

The bones of some of Doctor Graham's patients were discovered buried in the garden under the shrubs. Eight women were found alive in their rooms, too weak to move or speak. Not one could give a clear account of what had happened. They were sent home to recover as well as they could.

A couple of newspapers sent reporters to Mount Coffin. These inquisitive men roamed around for a while asking questions no one would answer. One of them stopped by our house and asked if we had known the Murder Doctor.

"No," said Eve Alice. "We keep to ourselves. So do most of our neighbors."

And she closed the door.

The soup that Granny and Mandy prepared for Doctor Graham became famous, too. It was called the Last Supper, which some people said was profane. The same people said a woman like the doctor ought not to get attention, even in death. Despite that opinion the story grew, but no one found out where the Last Supper came from. Everyone assumed the guilt-ridden Murder Doctor prepared it.

In the evening we continued to eat outside when the weather allowed. Olive would play hide-and-seek with Gilbert. Mandy and Eve Alice would talk about the old days. Mostly I sat near the women, listening and trying to learn all I could, while the crows sang their ragged song in the dark.

Months passed and I often dreamed of the women at the sanitarium. I would tell Granny what I dreamed, and we would cleanse the house and the land around it with sage and incantations. I thought of my grandmother's house as home, but I knew that our safety depended on these good habits.

One morning before dawn I woke up to the sound of splashing water. With my eyes still closed I imagined Olive was using the chamber pot, which she often did during the night. I drifted. I slept.

Light fell in pale strands across my pillow. I sat up in

bed. Livvy was gone. On her pillow lay the leather pouch she always wore around her neck, with the witch finger inside.

By now the mornings were quite cold. I scrambled into my sweater and shoes and climbed downstairs.

Outside the mist was starting to rise. Without knowing why I wandered away from the house. Instead of following the stream I walked directly into the woods where we were forbidden to go, in the direction opposite the chicken pen and outhouse and toward the sanitarium, which had been boarded up for months.

The ground was thick with weeds and sodden leaves. I stumbled a few times. I found the hat decorated with crow feathers lying in the mud.

I turned to make sure I could see our house, to get my bearings. I couldn't see it at all. I took another step into the forest and felt cold water surround my ankles.

Fog shifted between the trees and thinned just enough for me to spy a shallow pool of water among the ferns. In the icy water Olive lay face down, perfectly still, with her arms spread wide. Overhead a cedar branch shimmied and drops of water flew out and upward as a single crow sprang into the air.

The Changeling

I sold Eve Alice's house in the spring of 1935, a few weeks after she passed away in her sleep. I accepted the first offer, from a company buying up the timberland all around us. I had three good reasons for deciding to move. The first was the town itself.

By this time, the road in front of our house had been widened to accommodate trucks hauling timber. The stream where I used to fish had been drained for irrigation. A fence separated our backyard from the ravine.

In the 1920s a group of ladies from the local DAR circulated a petition to save what was left of Mount Coffin, as a historical site. They lost that battle and the blasting went on. Pretty soon the rock looked small and out of place sitting next to a sprawling mill. Most people considered a jagged spike of black rock sticking out of the ground to be an eyesore. They couldn't get rid of it fast enough.

Longview was pretty. Its brand new paved streets, train station, gardens and parks were carefully planned and assembled, a model town, in a v-shaped landmass between the Columbia and Cowlitz Rivers. Most of the people who lived there didn't know where the road-fill and gravel came from, and didn't care.

Doctor Graham's sanitarium was boarded up after the murders in 1912. For a while the new owners tried to turn it into a morbid tourist attraction. That idea went bust. Later a commercial farm bought the property. They knocked down what was left of the sanitarium. In its place they constructed a warehouse.

Eve Alice's friend Mandy was long dead. Gilbert had moved in with relatives in Portland.

Despite all the changes I might have gone on living in the new town of Longview, but two strange things happened after my grandmother died. The first was the arrival of a letter from my mother, addressed to Eve Alice. The second was the appearance of an unwanted visitor.

I decided to ignore Mama's letter begging Eve Alice to send 'the girls' to care for her in her 'final days.' I reasoned that she had gotten along well enough until now, so she could find help somewhere else. It crossed my mind that she wasn't thinking straight, since she couldn't even guess how old we might be. But I didn't feel a great desire to know the woman who described her life in such detail without asking how her daughters and her mother had fared.

I left the letter, all twenty pages, open on the kitchen table and went about my business. Around that time is when the dead women began to arrive.

From the day Mandy and Eve Alice had cooked their fateful supper for Doctor Graham, our families had paid tribute with sacrifices and rituals. My grandmother believed these would keep us safe. Olive's death was a terrible blow to Granny, and to me. Maybe it changed me in ways I don't know. After all of our tears, after all the grief, I was sure of this: To stray from the habits I had learned was to court something terrible just on the outskirts of our home. Something was drawn to every precious thing or person we loved, and looked upon us as Livvy and I had once looked through the window of Eve Alice's house, with yearning.

We went on sprinkling the rooms with lavender and rosemary. We swept each room from west to east, burned the dust and threw the ashes outdoors in the wind. These habits seemed to serve us, at least until Eve Alice died.

I moved into my grandmother's bedroom because I missed her and it comforted me to sleep there. I turned the mattress, added new sheets and pillows, and rearranged all of the potions and oils into a portable cabinet. I thanked the room and my grandmother for keeping me.

My first unwelcome visitor arrived at four in the morning. I heard a voice while I was sleeping. I woke in confusion with a tingling sensation along my arms. I sat up in the early gloom and felt a presence nearby. Something unsettled and separated from the darkness in the far corner. It moved toward me.

"Granny?" I said.

A woman I didn't recognize stepped toward me. Her body was mottled with bruises and mud. Her tangled braids hung down to her waist. The only garment she wore was a corset, twisted down around her hips. I didn't know her, but the jutting edges of her chin and collarbone, her wasted arms and legs, were unmistakable. The starveling gazed at me with swollen, hateful eyes.

I scrambled out of bed. I grabbed the box of matches off my bedside table and lit a candle. I turned toward the corner with the light. The woman was gone. There was nothing except a faint sickly smell of alcohol and fuchsia.

On the next night I heard water splashing. I went out to the old well. Two young women stood on the porch. Their hair lay over their shoulders knotted with ribbons. Their stained nightgowns clung to their skin. They were bruised, emaciated, with an air of resignation. They inclined their heads to one another, whispering.

"What do you want here?" I asked.

They entered the house. I followed them into the kitchen, but they were gone.

Sometimes I heard weeping in the middle of the day. Or I picked up the scent of cedar while I was cooking salmon. I might be hanging laundry on the line and notice that the back door was open, when I was sure I had closed it. Or I'd hear whispers and crying in my room at night, a shuffling sound at the foot of the bed.

No matter what I did to cleanse and put things right,

the spirits of the sanitarium wandered as they pleased. I didn't recognize them from the old newspaper photos and I reckoned they had never been found. When the sanitarium was closed down, the women there were sent home and some bodies were retrieved from the garden, but people always wondered. I was losing sleep, never able to predict when one of the wretched women might appear.

One afternoon I caught a glimpse of a plump girl dashing around the side of the house where the vine maple used to grow. I turned without thinking, hungry for a sight of my sister after all these years. And knowing full well that this couldn't be my Livvy, because we had buried her with love and honor, and remembered her with our tributes. We had not forgotten her.

I didn't know what being had taken the shape of my sister. I followed it past the kitchen window on my left, past the wood ferns, to the clothesline. I stopped there. The person standing next to the clothesline wasn't Olive. The blue dress and that placid expression took me back twenty-three years to the garden behind the sanitarium.

"We won't say a word about this, will we?" Said Doctor Graham, before the day's last sunlight struck through her and she disappeared.

For obvious reasons I decided to read Mama's letter again and consider paying her a visit. A second, close reading revealed that she was leaving her house, all of her belongings, and a small plot of land to her daughters, in other words to me.

I'm pretty sure I would never have heard from her again if she hadn't gotten sick. After so many years she finally wrote to Eve Alice mainly to say she was ill. Doctors couldn't help her any more. She was failing and wouldn't last long. Please, could the girls come and pay her a visit to say goodbye?

That was a hell of a thing, sitting alone at the kitchen table in Eve Alice's house, reading Mama's letter. I'll admit it. I wondered what my grandmother would have done, but this was just stalling. I knew she would have closed up the house or sold it and rushed to be with her only child.

The most surprising thing was the return address. I had to ask for a map at the Longview library. Even after I knew the letter's point of origin, I couldn't believe it.

Over the years I had imagined Mama in San Francisco or Chicago, or even New York, drinking champagne with a handsome man and dancing all night. One place I never pictured her was stuck in some nameless backwater less than forty miles from where she dropped us off to live with our grandmother.

She'd had plans the night she left us: New automobile, new city, new clothes, new name, and a career doing something that drew a lot of attention and didn't require much effort, whatever that might be. But John Dee had plans, too. He was tired of supporting Mama. He was already married to a middle-aged woman who owned a horse ranch in Coeur d'Alene. He broke the news to Mama when he dropped her off several miles east of the Cowlitz River.

Too embarrassed to make her way back to Mount Coffin, she worked in the front office at a cannery for almost a year and then married the foreman. They were all right together, but she said the foreman had a temper. They settled into the house he built, a snug little bungalow by the railroad tracks (with more room, she said, and better conveniences than Eve Alice's 'rattling old place'). After that she didn't dare tell the foreman what she'd been doing before he appeared. She never found the moment or the nerve to break the news that she'd had a family long before he came to her rescue.

That was her story. I let her hold onto it because by the time I knew her she didn't have long to live. Her saga went on:

She'd had nine good years of marriage. Then the foreman had died of a stroke and left her the house and a scrap of land but no money to live on. She drew upon what she had learned from Eve Alice as a child and began supplying remedies and elixirs to the women she knew.

One night a teenaged girl came to see her. The girl said she worked at the cannery but everybody knew she took money for sleeping with men in the logging camps. She was in trouble and she had heard Mama knew what to do.

"Go to a doctor," Mama told her. "That's a lot safer than what I can offer."

"That bastard won't do what I need him to do." The girl was crying. She said she was getting by the only way she knew how, and if nobody would help her she might as well throw herself in the river.

I could say Mama helped the girl out of pity but that would be the same lie she told. Pity wouldn't have cost anything. For a few dollars she made up a tin of herbs and spices for the girl to drink as a tea. This was Eve Alice's recipe. I recognized the combination of carrot seed, nutmeg, and mugwort she described in the exact proportions my grandmother had used for years.

Mama told the girl to drink the tea every six hours, even if she had to wake up in the middle of the night for a dose. She had to sip the tea while taking a hot bath. Mama recommended long walks too, the more strenuous the better.

A week later the girl came back to say thank you. Once the flow started she'd kept her blood in a jar the way Mama suggested. That way she could see that her period had flushed her womb clean. But she said she didn't talk to it, the way she was supposed to, and Mama asked her why not.

"Talking to it won't make any difference, will it?" The girl asked. "It's nothing but guilt that makes people pray, and I don't feel bad at all."

That night Mama lit candles in the kitchen and in her bedroom. She got down on her knees and spoke to the spirit she had helped the girl wash from her body.

"We all come to this world and wait on the doorstep. Now is not the time for you. Release us. We beg your forgiveness. Release us..."

Then she cleansed the house. She walked all around the outside, too, repeating the words.

Before Doctor Graham had a chance to return for a visit I sold the house and gave away most of what I owned. It wasn't much. With every intention of leaving the rock of the dead behind me, I moved to the east side of the Cowlitz River to care for my mother and to start over.

Imagine my surprise when I arrived in a town so neglected and so often ignored by travelers that it didn't have an official name. In fact it wasn't a town yet, only a scattering of cabins, bungalows, farms, and makeshift logging camps. Its main distinction was its proximity to a railroad station, one that was built for the shipment of Douglas fir, not the comfort of passengers.

Mama's house was every bit as small as Eve Alice's. The difference was that its modern kitchen, two tidy bedrooms and bathroom were all on one floor. The kitchen had screens on the front door and windows, so I could see the front yard and the road while eating.

The bathroom was heaven-sent. Eve Alice had tried to add a bathroom to the back porch the year before she died, but it never worked out. We still used the well for drinking water. Keeping fresh water and sewage separate meant the best place for a bathroom was where the outhouse stood. So after much talk the idea was abandoned altogether.

The woman who opened the screen door to greet me when I arrived was a far cry from the one I remembered. Her hair was still black as night, though it had lost its luster. She was heavyset and the glint of mischief in her eyes had gone. Her lips used to curl at the corners whenever she said something funny. Now they were set in a kind of sneer, as if she didn't expect one thing to happen that wouldn't be a disappointment. Including me, I guess. She looked me up and down skeptically, as though she suspected I had killed and eaten her daughter instead of simply growing up.

"Delphine?" She asked.

I nodded. I showed her the little leather pouch I still wore around my neck. She recognized her mother's handiwork, so she let me in.

I could pretend we made up, and told stories, and cried. I could say she died in my arms after a heartfelt reunion. But it wasn't like that. I made coffee. I unpacked my clothes. I told her that Eve Alice and Olive might visit later on. I didn't see any reason to cause her more pain.

She told me more about her life. She didn't ask any questions about mine, and I didn't offer because she was the one who was dying.

With help she was able to walk in the yard from the bungalow to the road and back, but only for a couple more days. The last three weeks she was bedridden. After that she seemed to decline more with every hour.

She got bored and restless and sick of having me clean up after her, sick of using the bedpan. She had been a fastidious woman all of her life, and she wasn't going to change in her final days.

"We've got an indoor commode," she said.

"I know."

"Not a damn outhouse up in the woods."

"I know. But getting you from the bed to the commode is the problem now. You want me to drag you in there on a rug?"

"No!"

"I'll do that if you want me to."

"No!"

In the last week she stopped drinking the vegetable broth I prepared and then she stopped drinking water. All she would accept was the herbal tea that took the worst of the pain away. Then, as she drifted, she would enter the past recalling this year or that as though she were trying different doors, opening one and looking out, then closing it and moving on to another.

"I've got to get away from this pokey old town," she said once.

She looked up from the bed and fixed me with her dull eyes. For a second she recognized me, not as I was but as I had been. She spoke to me as she had all those years ago.

"You're the hard one," she told me. "Olive is pretty, like me. She has a good soul, too."

I kept my mouth shut. I didn't say what year it was. I let her think Olive was alive, a happy girl living on moonlight and lullabies. What difference did it make?

Now and then she had a lucid moment. She would call me by name and speak to me, one woman to another:

"This house is yours, Delphine. I wrote it in my will and it's signed by a notary."

"Well, that's something," I said.

Then I poured her another cup of tea. She was fading and she would be gone in another day or so. All I could offer was a brew that would take the edge off the pain and let her drift instead of crawling toward the end.

"You were never mine," she said. "You were my mother's granddaughter, but never my daughter."

"I know."

"You'll never have a husband," she told me.

"Not after the ones I've seen," I said, and smiled.

And she slept. I don't know if she dreamed. Her face was calm and her hands lay still across her stomach. A few hours later she woke up to tell me:

"Olive is the soft one. She has a good figure. You can see that."

I didn't remind her that the last time she'd seen Olive she was eight years old: Eight and dressed in her only outfit, a dowdy yellow cotton dress and threadbare coat, waving goodbye.

"Oh!" She said.

I took her hand and brushed the hair back from her forehead.

"Oh, me," she said.

She opened her eyes wide for a second and looked straight at me.

"I'm going to have to die, honey."

When she drew her last breath and sighed and lay still I thought I would cry. But I didn't. I held onto her hand. Later I curled her hair and washed her face and used a brush to clean the bits of dust off her best dress, a violet shift with a bit of white flowers embroidered on one shoulder.

The house I inherited appeared to be in good condition over all. The foundation was solid. The plumbing was sound. I discovered a few spots where Mama's husband had taken shortcuts and I had to improvise repairs. He had put down some tiles in the bathroom, and got most of them crooked. Little things. The yard was a mess but there was enough room for a garden and a beehive and a few trees.

One problem was insulation. The woodwork was flimsy in places. Mama had called her husband a real handyman, but he had worked in a cannery instead of a lumberyard for good reason. At first I took care not to harm the original finish on what proved to be cheap wood. To my mind, keeping warm in winter was more important than beauty. In later years, when I had more than myself to consider, if I felt a draught in January I didn't think twice about nailing a rug or two to the wall.

Now I'm getting ahead of my story. And everything relies on telling it as well and as honestly as I can.

A few months after I moved into Mama's house the town acquired its name. A local businessman decided it should be Skillute, which he claimed had come to him in a dream. Another part of his dream was that Skillute would be 'free,' placing no limits on land use. Anyone could build just about anything so long as his neighbors didn't object enough to sue him. Soon after the town leadership approved these measures, the same businessman put up billboards advertising his company's latest product, a tractor with a two-cylinder engine.

My life in Skillute was often solitary, although many people came and went: wives of loggers, farmers, and ranch hands; women who worked at the grocery store and the beauty salon; cleaning women, diner cooks, and schoolteachers. In most cases I was able to help them in one way or another. Some needed healing, but most were not sick. A pot of soothing chamomile and two hours of sympathetic conversation had a remarkable effect. Over the years I added palm reading and harmless predictions, which proved to be popular so long as the predictions were optimistic. And I helped a few women who were in trouble, ones who would have been on their own otherwise.

One way I was able to add to my income was to barter as Eve Alice did. While she had traded eggs and string beans and lettuce, I matched up people who needed things but didn't know where to find them. I matched up a widowed farmer with a romantic secretary. I introduced a tailor who couldn't feed his family and a bride whose parents ran a dairy farm and would pay a good price for a fine wedding dress. In every instance I would benefit just a tiny bit from both sides of the arrangement. I got by in this way for many years.

Healthy for most of my youth, in my late forties I began to feel my age. I had a touch of arthritis I treated with ginger root tea and rosemary. For the first time, though, I knew what it was to face old age alone. I wasn't about to marry and I was too old to have a child. I wondered what would happen someday if I couldn't earn my keep. By this time I had a beat-up '46 Chevy coupe that could just about do forty-five miles an hour on flat road if there wasn't a breeze. So I got around pretty well. But I wondered what the future would bring.

One of the families I met in the 1950s lived in a cabin five miles from my house. The help I gave to the Dempseys was pure charity. They were part of a larger clan that had migrated west during the Depression. This branch of the family had never prospered. The husband drifted and complained. The wife was sick more often than she was well. The first time I met the Dempseys their youngest child, Flora, was twelve.

The boys of the family were always wandering. They would take a job, earn a paycheck, and stop showing up. Or an accident would occur and they would claim an injury. 'Shiftless' is what most people called them.

The day I introduced myself to Mrs. Dempsey and left her with a remedy for her headache, three boys were sitting on the front steps of the tin-roofed shack smoking pipes. Only one of the three moved aside as I made my way down the steps. He said:

"What's she got?"

"Your mother?" I asked.

The one who had spoken stared at me with cornflower blue eyes. He didn't answer. I didn't feel a need to tell him his mother's business.

"She ought to feel better soon," I told him.

Mr. Dempsey sidled up alongside me. He wiped his face with a bandana and handed me a nickel.

"You don't owe me anything," I said.

"Nothing's free," he said. "I'm busy working all day long keeping this house together."

Everybody knew the family didn't own the house or rent it. They occupied it because otherwise it stood empty while the absent owners decided what to do with it.

The garden looked parched. A married son and his wife and kids were living in an Army tent in the yard, and a toddler sauntered across the yard naked. The boys who were smoking on the front steps finally stood up when their younger sister Flora stepped out of the shack. I wondered where she had been while I was visiting with her mother, and despite her age I thought, even then, she was strange.

She was thin and brittle. Her blond hair was filthy, with bits of leaves and weeds stuck in it. She wore a dress that might have been re-sewn from one of her father's shirts.

"Come on, girl," the boy with cornflower eyes began to tease.

Flora tried to get past him. She held a doll's head in both hands, and kept it close to her chest. He snatched up the doll's head and handed it to the next boy, who held it up just beyond her reach.

"It's right here! Flora! Come get it!"

The girl clambered up his legs, grasping at him with both hands. She screamed in frustration, and pounded her brother's legs with her fists.

"Giiiiiiive!"

At the moment she reached her full rage the third brother reached down and grabbed her by her ankles. He dangled her in the air upside down. Then the other two boys poked and prodded, tickling her, while their mother shouted from the doorway for them to stop.

I witnessed this game again the next time I brought a tonic for Mrs. Dempsey. I wondered what the boys got up to when there were no outsiders around.

On that second visit I asked Mrs. Dempsey if she would be willing to let Flora come to my house during the day to help me with this and that around the house. Maybe I could teach her a little about making remedies, and I could pay her a quarter every week. Mrs. Dempsey agreed right away. She even made an effort to clean her daughter's clothes and brush her hair for her new 'job.' The girl still wasn't much to look at but I thought if she learned how to tend to the sick, and especially if she took to me, I might have an apprentice I could count on later in life. This was a selfish plan, one that would come back to haunt me, but it seemed innocent enough back then.

Flora seemed eager to learn. Whether I was mixing herbs or sweeping the floor she watched me as if her life depended on every move I made. Her gaunt face was made even thinner by her habit of sucking her cheeks in when she was concentrating. She would fix an object— a sewing needle, a faucet, or a beehive, it made no difference— with that stare of hers, and she wouldn't look away until I called out her name. I thought her concentration showed that she was taking everything in.

Within a month I realized my mistake. Self-education calls for a certain curiosity. Curiosity is different from hunger. What Flora had was an animal hunger, a yearning that wouldn't be satisfied, because she couldn't understand how things fit together.

She had never learned to read, either in school or at home. I sat down with her many times and tried to teach her the alphabet. Her mind was so neglected that none of it made sense to her.

She couldn't remember the steps to a task. If I told her to sweep the porch she knew to pick up the broom but she never knew where to begin sweeping. She might start at the edges and work her way to the middle, or sweep in a circle and then back the other direction. One time she swept all the dust off the porch into the house, and then lay down on the kitchen floor and fell asleep.

As long as I said she was doing all right, she was fine. If I gave any sign that she was wrong, she would lose all her patience at once. She only had enough willpower to stick with an activity as long as it was going well. Any problem or mistake or change of plan would throw her off. Then she would have a tantrum, pulling at her hair and clothes and yelling gibberish until she was worn out and sleepy.

"I don't believe the girl is stupid," I told Kitty Johnson, who was one of my regulars.

"Maybe her brain is impaired," said Kitty. She sipped coffee and through the screen door watched Flora tossing weeds around the yard.

"No," I told her. "It's just that nobody's ever asked her to make sense, or follow rules. No one ever taught her to do one thing until she mastered it. That's how you get confidence."

"Delphine," she said. "There's no telling how much time she's spent alone, maybe even locked up."

"Her family treats her the way they would treat a cat or a dog they found."

"Well," she said. "It's no surprise, then. Poor thing. How old is she, again?"

By the second month I knew the arrangement I'd made would never work out. No matter how patiently I explained, Flora still wasn't learning. It was more trouble than it was worth having her with me. By the end of the day I was too tired to move. I wondered how I could get out of my agreement with the girl's mother without offending her and without leaving Flora to the mercy of her siblings.

This was the very moment when Harriet Knox came into my life. I thought many times since how strange it was that our paths crossed, but now I know it was hardly by accident.

There was a lot of enthusiasm in the decade following the Second World War. The Interstate freeway was under construction. We had a post office. There was a new train station that catered to passengers instead of cargo. A couple of doctors had hung out their shingle, taking away part of my clientele, but also offering better health and modern medicine to a town sorely in need.

The Department of Transportation brought an engineer named William Robert Knox from Boston to oversee the building of the freeway in our part of the state. He was important enough to have his picture in the local newspaper, and everyone commented on what a handsome man he was. They wondered what his wife must be like.

Maybe it was the car, an Oldsmobile painted a color I would have called yellow, but I later learned was 'Canto Cream.' It had clean whitewall tires and white upholstery. I had never seen anything like it, but suddenly one morning in mid-September it was parked in front of my house.

Maybe it was the woman herself, standing on my doorstep in a smart dress suit. The gold-rust color of her outfit showed off her red hair. She wore brown gloves and her brown leather purse matched her shoes. When I first set eyes on her I thought I must have dozed off at the kitchen table and started to dream I was somewhere far from Skillute.

"Are you Mrs. Dodd?" The woman asked through the screen door.

"Yes," I said. It was my habit to let people think what they liked about my past, as long as it wasn't anything terrible. If most people wanted to see me as a genteel widow, so be it.

"How do you do, Mrs. Dodd," she said. "I am Mrs. William Knox. I've come to you for a consultation."

I opened the screen door. In the full light she was like a picture in a fashion magazine.

She pulled off one of her gloves and shook my hand delicately, pinching my calloused fingers with her pale manicured ones. Her nails were painted crimson to match her lipstick. She drew a halting breath and dabbed the corners of her hazel eyes with a tiny silk handkerchief. When she was done she returned the handkerchief to her purse before she said:

"I was referred by my cleaning lady, Kitty Johnson. She recommended you in glowing terms."

Flora sat in a patch of sunlight near the house, picking at the weeds and flowers she had pulled loose. I'd given up asking her to help around the house.

Harriet smiled when she saw the girl but didn't ask if she was mine.

That morning I was glad I had replaced a few pieces of Mama's old furniture. The kitchen was bright white and yellow, with a new percolator and a modern stove. The table and chairs were secondhand but in good condition. I still didn't have a telephone. I drove down the road to the post office if I had to make a call but that was always tricky. Since we were on a party line I might have to wait half an hour. The postmistress made good use of the time by charging people a nickel for a cup of coffee.

Mrs. Knox and I sat opposite one another over slices of a cake I'd baked the day before. She glanced around, taking the place in without gawking, and said:

"You have such a sweet home."

This unsettled me a bit. I hadn't thought about where I lived since I was a child in Eugene. Suddenly I wondered what my house was worth, and whether it had cost as much to build as the Oldsmobile sitting in front of it.

Mrs. Knox said she wanted a consultation but when I offered to read her palm she said she didn't care for that. I asked if she had a physical ailment and she said no.

"Not exactly."

It was my habit to let each woman tell me what she felt was wrong, instead of putting words in her mouth. Plenty of other people did that and sometimes it was the cause of the problem in the first place.

"My doctor thinks I'm a fool," she said. "He's prescribed Miltown. My friends take it. My doctor is happy to let me have as much as I need. For what he charges I'm not surprised."

"Are you taking the tranquilizers?" I asked.

"No. Not anymore. They made me feel strange, as though I were sleepwalking, or walking underwater. Do you know what I mean?"

I nodded.

"Everyone thinks I should calm down. I feel so restless all day. My husband had a charming cottage built for us, a temporary place he can sell when his work assignment ends. We have a garden. And all of the conveniences, as they say. Bill thinks I should be completely happy there."

"But you're not?"

She laughed.

"Oh, you should see it! Stupid thing, it's bright blue with white shutters and a flagstone walkway. It sits at the end of a gravel drive in the middle of nowhere, surrounded by trees and shrubbery. All that's missing are bluebirds singing all day. Honestly, it's like something out of a Loretta Young movie. It's ridiculous!"

I must have looked surprised.

She went on to say:

"Mrs. Dodd, I have a degree in art history from one of the best schools in New York. Well, that's nothing, now. I mean, it doesn't guarantee anything, does it? Life is unpredictable. What did my father always say? 'Count your blessings.' My husband is doing well. My husband has a career he likes. My husband wants children."

She looked away. Then she took a sip of coffee.

"What about you, Mrs. Knox? Do you want to have children?"

"I had a miscarriage a few months ago. That stupid doctor told me to try again right away. Suddenly it seems very complicated, this mundane thing that everyone can do. I don't know. I always expected a family would just happen. Why not? Every woman I know has a family or plans to have one. I'm perfectly healthy. My friend Mrs. Cartwright says you know some secrets, or home remedies. And Kitty said— But, look, I'm not going to kiss a frog or, I don't know, swallow flies to conceive a child."

I couldn't help laughing.

"My methods are the same ones my grandmother and her grandmother used," I explained. "It's just a few herbs and common sense. I can't make you pregnant. Only your husband can do that, if he's able to and if you're able to. And if that's what you want."

Now she laughed, too. It was a bright sound like the jingling of a tiny bell.

"It isn't a matter of not being able," she said. "Believe me. My husband is entirely capable. But he has an important job, and sometimes he's gone for two or three weeks at a time. For example, I haven't seen him in twelve days."

Her eyes took in the room again. I couldn't tell what

she wanted from me.

"Mrs. Knox."

"Please, call me Harriet."

"Harriet, what does your doctor say?"

"That quack! He gives me the willies. I'm through with these old men telling me what's wrong with my mind. He tells me to calm down, and then he tells me to stay busy. I am busy. I'm always busy. I have things to do. I have my bridge club and the women's club. Pardon me, do you mind if I smoke?"

I fetched an ashtray and she lit up a cigarette. She went on:

"I have planning committees and dinner parties. If anything I have too much to do. No. I need something worthwhile, a project that matters, something that isn't about me, and my silly girlfriends. Do you understand?"

I thought I understood but she was so hard to read. In fact Harriet Knox was the most peculiar woman I had ever met. By this time there were quite a few well-heeled wives in Skillute, women who had followed their husbands and their jobs, but she was the first I had seen up close. When she exhaled she tilted her head back and let the smoke roll upward and away from the table. Her thoughts, too, seemed to come quickly and then roll away, as though she didn't want them.

"I do expect to have a child one day," she said. "Of course. But what I need now is to care for someone, to be needed."

"You might volunteer to visit people who are old or sick," I said.

She looked away, sighed, and said:

"Have you ever heard the old wives' tale about pregnancy inspired by adoption?"

"Yes, but I don't know if it's true," I said. "I read that in a magazine but I'm not sure I believe it."

"I've seen it happen a few times," she told me.

"So you want to adopt a child?"

She frowned.

"I don't think I want to adopt another woman's problem. No, I don't mean it like that. A woman only gives her baby away if there's something wrong. She might not say it, but she has an instinct, doesn't she? You have to wonder."

"Then what do you have in mind?" I asked.

"I feel useless, Mrs. Dodd. I've never felt so useless in my life. I only thought maybe I could find a child in need, a girl who has potential, and take her under my wing for a little while."

"A girl?"

"Yes. Don't you think that's a good idea?"

She smiled brightly. She took a draw on her cigarette and waited.

"Not a little boy?" I asked.

"Um," she began and paused to gather her thoughts. "Boys need a man around the house, don't you think? When his assignment here is done, my husband and I will settle down, have dinner at home every night, take our holidays together, that sort of thing. But right now it's just me at home, you see, and I think I would be more inspiring to a young girl."

"Well," I said. "It seems like you know your own mind."

"The trouble is, we are still new in town and I just don't know where to begin. I wonder if you know someone who could really benefit from my help. I desperately want to be of use to someone, Mrs. Dodd."

A catch in her voice made me think I ought to help her. I'm ashamed to say it. I can't even say why I felt that way.

"Call me Delphine," I told her. "The person I know who's most in need of help might be hard on your nerves."

"Oh," she said. "I like a challenge. I don't expect this to be easy, not at all. I want to make a real difference, you see."

"I know a poor family," I said. "The youngest child is named Flora, she's about twelve."

In the corner of my eye a shadow moved against the light. I turned and saw that Flora was standing right up

78

against the screen door on the outside, staring in. She didn't say anything. She was so close to the door that I couldn't see her face at all, only the shape of her.

"Flora!" I shouted. "Don't eavesdrop, now. Go and play."

After a few seconds Flora backed away from the door.

Harriet tilted her head, briefly lost in her thoughts. Then she said:

"Is this the girl you're suggesting, Delphine? The girl I saw outside?"

"Flora Dempsey is her full name. You can see that she's a handful. I haven't made much progress with her."

"I understand," said Harriet. "And I'd like to see what a tutor, a music teacher, a new wardrobe, and three square meals a day could do for that girl. Wouldn't you?"

Outside the sun was faltering. It would be another overcast day, after all.

"I would," I said.

She beamed. The way she smiled, she might have been a movie star on a USO tour.

"Perfect," she said. "Delphine, you are a godsend."

Eve Alice would have advised me to think hard about this friendship. With the dawning of my fear of old age a woman appeared and soon made my life more secure and comfortable than it had been before. What she proposed to do solved a problem I had created. Eve Alice would have asked why, but that was because she herself had been tempted by ease and comfort and had given in for a while. This is the nature of temptation, you see. If it didn't come in the exact form we desire, we would never consider it. All it takes to indulge in what we want is to turn a blind eye now and then.

Flora's father was happy to have a woman he had never met take his daughter off his hands once she offered a hundred dollars to compensate for his concern. That's how desperate the man was.

Matching Flora Dempsey with a woman who viewed

her as both a charity case and a distraction had the side benefit of buying me a corner of Harriet's world. She introduced me to three of her friends, who insisted on paying for readings. They gave me extravagant gifts when my remedies brought relief from their phantom ailments. I had never felt like a fraud before, and I had never lived so well.

I bought new tires for the Chevy. I painted the house and paid a man to clear the blackberry bushes from the yard. I planted vine maples along the side of the house.

William Knox was a handsome man. His newspaper photograph didn't do him justice. He was over six feet tall and broad-shouldered with a quick smile and a head of thick, black hair. All of which offset the delicacy of his eyes, by turns gray or violet depending on the light. His manner showed confidence just shy of arrogance. I imagined this came from being recognized in his field, and popular among both men and women. He wasn't rude or unkind but he made it clear that he didn't see how anyone with good health and intelligence could fail at whatever they set out to do. I could see right away that his wife's dissatisfaction made no sense to him.

I watched the two of them go through what Harriet called 'our usual routine' one day when I delivered a batch of ginger tea and honey. We sat down in the living room. Harriet said Mr. Knox was upstairs packing his suitcases for another trip.

"Take the damn car and drive up the coast with one of your girlfriends!" He shouted.

"I've seen the coast!" Harriet shouted back. "I have plans today!"

"Why don't you ever go to the country club? Go to Longview. Just don't sit around!"

"You think all I do is sit around! For God's sake, I'm not Bonnie Cartwright!"

His voice still boomed at us when he stepped into the living room. He put his suitcases on the floor.

"Oh, fine. What's wrong with Bonnie, now?" He asked.

"Did I say anything was wrong?"

"If you could stop obsessing about your friends and actually do something, you would feel better."

"I'm painting the spare bedroom for Flora today."

He was silent for a moment. Then he picked up his suitcases and carried them to the front door.

Harriet got up and left the room. I could hear the two of them talking in the hall.

"I've arranged it. The least you can do is thank me."

"I didn't ask you to do this," he said. Then he mentioned wasting time with Ouija boards and voodoo. And he left.

Harriet invited me over more often. She paid me to advise her friends at her home once a week. It was sort of a party for women only. They were all in their late twenties and early thirties, immaculately coifed and groomed. They all had nicknames: Killjoy, Bunny, Slim, Goldilocks, and Charles (for Charlotte). Some were silly and polite, but the one they called Slim always referred to me as 'the witch' when she thought I wasn't listening.

"You're not really going to bring a twelve-year-old charity case into the house, are you?" She asked Harriet.

"Of course I am."

"You're making your own bed," Slim told her.

She followed Harriet to the living room and the hall and back while she picked up the ashtrays after one of their parties. I tidied up the kitchen and barely resisted the urge to count the stash of money in my purse, a hand-tooled cowhide bag Harriet had given me.

"And you'll have to lie in it."

"What do you mean?" Harriet said.

"You know exactly I mean."

"I'm sure I don't."

"This isn't going to solve anything. What are you thinking?"

"She's a poor little child from a miserable family and I can brighten her life. Why shouldn't I?"

"Are you out of your mind, Harriet?"

"It's a perfectly reasonable thing to do. And I don't like your insinuations."

"All right," said Slim. "Let's look at the other side of it."

"What side?"

"Suppose she has lice, or, I don't know, rickets! What if she steals?"

"Dear God," Harriet laughed. "What if she's a Martian? The things you think of, Slim!"

"You have time to reconsider. Just give her family some money and be done with it."

"Why is this any of your business?"

"Fine," said Slim. "If that's the way it is. But I warn you: Don't come to me when this gets ugly. I wash my hands of it right this minute. Don't ask me for help."

Talking Mrs. Dempsey into the arrangement with Harriet was harder than I expected. Now I can see that I assumed she would be happy to send Flora to another woman's home full-time for a few months, because giving a daughter away didn't seem entirely unnatural to me. I even looked down on the woman for not giving Flora the chance to do better than she had done.

"It's only for a little while," I told her.

The liquid light in her eyes spoke for her. She didn't believe me.

"You want Flora to learn," she said. "Why don't you teach her? Let her work with you, like my husband said, and get her to know medicine and whatnot like you do."

"Mrs. Dempsey," I explained. "Mrs. Knox and her husband are very well off. Their home may be small..."

At this she sort of laughed and shook her head. That was the first time I realized I was taking on Harriet's measure of the world. Her home wasn't small. It was a large and luxurious imitation of a small country home.

"I can't offer you anything," I told Mrs. Dempsey. "They can give you a hundred dollars, and your daughter will have a good life."

At these words her husband, who was supposed to be working in the yard, stepped into the shack. He pointed at the rusting tin roof and the wormholes in the unpainted walls.

"When you think of a way that's better than this, you say so," he told her.

After that she didn't argue. She turned away from me, away from her husband, away from Flora, and concentrated on a point somewhere past the window and the yard. She never spoke to me again.

Once her father delivered her to Harriet's house, collected his fee, and left, Flora appeared to stop fighting the idea. She slumped in one of the living room chairs while I tried to drag a brush through her matted blond hair.

"Now, Flora," Harriet said to her. "This will be your home for a while. There's no need to be frightened. Your family is right where you left them and you can visit them once in a while, so they won't worry about you. I hear you don't go to school. I've hired a tutor to come here in the afternoons and a piano teacher will come twice a week."

Flora said nothing. Her dull eyes scanned the room.

"The first order of business is to get you cleaned up and buy you some nice clothes. Would you like that?"

Flora stared at Harriet.

Harriet said to me:

"This must be confusing for her. That's understandable. Poor wretch."

On the word 'wretch' Flora's whole body shifted forward. She looked up at Harriet with more interest now. I was foolish enough to take this as a good sign.

For the next two weeks I didn't hear from Harriet. I tried calling her from the post office. Every time I finally got a line out the phone rang and rang until the operator cut me off.

Another week went by. Finally one day the cleaning woman, Kitty, answered and said the lady of the house was too busy to talk at the moment.

"Kitty," I said. "This is Delphine. I want to find out how Flora's doing."

There was a long silence.

"Kitty?"

"I'm sure Mrs. Knox and Miss Knox are fine," she said.

"Miss Knox?"

"That's what the lady of the house told me, and that's all I can say."

The line went dead. When I tried again there was no answer. So I wrapped up a jar of honey as an excuse and went over to visit unannounced.

The wrought iron gate to the front yard was unlatched. The Oldsmobile was nowhere to be seen. The house stood silent and still.

Harriet was right. Every time I saw the house the robin's egg blue paint and white shutters reminded me of a storybook or a movie. Maple leaves wafted down and swept across the yard like tiny flying carpets. I walked up the flagstone path and knocked on the door. I waited quite a while, until the floorboards squeaked and the door opened with a sort of sigh.

Harriet stood inside the hall. I had to take a step into the house before I could see her face. Her jaw was clenched and her eyes were accented with dark circles. She had told me she often had trouble sleeping. One of the remedies I provided was a mixture of valerian, anise, and ginger.

As I stepped forward Harriet seemed to draw back into shadow. My eyes adjusted to the change of light and I could see that she had a small, deep gash in her left temple. She had cleaned and dried the wound and added a dab of Mercurochrome.

"How did this happen?" I asked.

She flinched when I raised my hand toward her face. I noticed, too, that her lips were raw as though she had been chewing them.

"Bill says I'm the clumsiest woman he's ever known. I

think I could injure myself drinking a glass of water."

She picked up a pack of cigarettes from the hall table. I followed her into the living room and sat down while she paced, smoking.

"How did you get that cut on your face?"

"Honestly, Delphine, don't you have a potion to make me more graceful?"

"Is your husband home?" I asked.

"No," she said.

"How is Flora doing?"

"Oh," she said. "As well as we have any right to expect. Poor thing."

Her voice was completely flat. She sat on the couch and finished her cigarette without looking at me while we talked.

"What does the tutor think? Is Flora learning anything?"

Harriet laughed, more of an eruption like a sudden sneeze. There wasn't any mirth in it.

"I paid the woman a bonus and let her go after the first week. It was an act of mercy."

"Are you going to send Flora to school?"

"Didn't you know? She isn't allowed to go. Our little darling flunked out of school years ago, and the principal is adamant about not having her return. Just one of the things her father never mentioned. Always read the fine print, eh?"

I noticed that all of the downstairs lights were out. Barely enough autumn sun strayed through the windows so that I could see Harriet's face. She was pale and the circles under her eyes made her resemble an animal in the half-shadows.

On most of the days when I had visited before there was music throughout the house. Harriet liked to play records in the afternoon, and while playing cards. Now it appeared that she was alone in the house. I listened closely but I didn't hear a sound.

"What is she up to now?" I asked.

"The little beast is probably messing around upstairs, looking for trouble," she said.

"Isn't this your bridge club day?"

"No, not any more. I have my hands full. So much to do!"

She stubbed out her cigarette in a lacquered ashtray on the table. Then she stood smartly and held out one hand to guide me toward the door.

"Thanks awfully for stopping by," she said.

"Is there anything I can do?" I asked as I stepped across the threshold into the gray and golden light outdoors.

"No, dear," she said just before she closed and locked the door. "You've been such a help. I think you've done enough."

The next day I happened to have a consultation with a regular, Gloria, a young woman who had recently gotten a job cooking for Bonnie Cartwright on special occasions. After I'd read Gloria's palm she stayed on to have a cup of tea with me. She claimed that Mrs. Cartwright and Harriet were no longer on speaking terms.

"They didn't seem to be close friends to begin with," I said.

"Well, I don't know," said Gloria. "But this is about the girl she's taken in. Mrs. C won't have her in the house."

Gloria went on to say that Harriet had been introducing the girl, smartly dressed and manicured, as Miss Flora Knox. Harriet's friends were as polite as they could manage to be, until a few things went missing: a bracelet, a change purse, a bottle of perfume. When Harriet asked Flora if she had stolen things while they visited her friends, the girl threw a tantrum and broke a mirror on the wall in Harriet's bedroom. That was when things got bad.

"How do you mean?" I asked.

"Not sure," said Gloria, helping herself to more cake. "See, Kitty and I used to be real good friends. She told me Mrs. K was crazy."

"Why would she say that?"

"See, I don't know, because Mrs. K made her stop talking to me. Said if she found out she was gossiping she would get fired. Kitty's a nice girl, and she needs the money to help her mom and dad."

"Yes," I said. "Well, what else does Bonnie Cartwright say?"

"She said Mrs. K called Mr. K and they had an argument. He said the problem was all Harriet's fault because she chose the girl. Then Mrs. K said that was a hell of a thing to say, after they had to move all the way across the country and she gave up everything for him. I guess there was some trouble back in Boston, but I don't know what. Mr. K told her to shut up, and she told him he had to punish the girl when he came home because she couldn't do a thing with her."

"How did Bonnie Cartwright hear about this?"

"Oh, eavesdropping on the telephone, of course. See, Mrs. C's husband is in sales and he's on the road a lot. She likes to sniff around and find out what people are up to. Only now she won't speak to Mrs. K because of the girl."

"I don't understand."

"Mrs. C said something about Harriet being un-something."

"Unhappy?"

"No. It was more— unstable? No. Unwholesome. That's what she said."

"But how can she make that claim? I don't think they're close friends at all."

"They used to be," said Gloria. "They went to school together when they were little girls, and all the way up through college. Mrs. C said Mrs. K has been seeing a doctor since she was fifteen."

"For what?"

"Her head. Her father sent her to a psychiatrist. He made her go, and she didn't like it one bit, but her father said if she didn't go he was cutting her out of the family. She kept on seeing a head doctor until right before she got married."

"Bonnie Cartwright told you all of this?"

"Oh, heck, no. I heard her talking on the telephone a couple times with that gal they call Slim— weird name for a lady, don't you think?"

I didn't know what to do. Whenever I called Harriet no one answered. Some people might have gone to the sheriff's office but I didn't. They might have asked questions about the women who came to see me, and the kind of services I offered. I hate to admit it but this was on my mind. I felt responsible, too, for making the deal between the Dempseys and Harriet Knox. I needed to get back in touch, to find out what was happening between Harriet and Flora. So I spent a little money and had my first telephone installed.

Most of the things I learned by listening in on the party line were useless. The postmistress was thinking of upping the price of coffee to a dime. Old Man Sanders had gone crazy again and shot the family dog. Mrs. Jasper was planning a trip to visit her sister in Kelso.

I discovered that late in the evening was when Harriet placed calls to her husband. These were brief chats and less enlightening than I hoped.

"Did I wake you?"

"Of course not."

"Will you be home on Tuesday?"

"Unlikely. We've had to fire two men and I have to stay until the new team shows up."

They never expressed affection. Harriet alternated between agitation and drowsiness. William was always the same. He couldn't say goodbye soon enough. One time, though, he asked:

"Where is the girl?"

The pause that followed could have swallowed Skillute whole. Finally Harriet said:

"She's in her room. No doubt tearing holes in the dress I bought her today."

"You go overboard."

"If I have to be seen with her I want her to be presentable."

"Tell yourself that's the reason."

"Because it is."

"All right," he said. "All right. Fine. I have to go."

The next time I saw Harriet she was completely unlike the woman I had met in the early autumn, the woman in a smart suit driving a handsome car. On the outside she was Harriet: She wore a gold silk dress with full skirt, matching belt, and black pumps, and her red hair was swept up into a French bun. But her makeup was brash and overdone. I wondered if she was hiding more sleepless nights, or worse.

She stood at the front door to her house shouting Flora's name. Shortly the girl came into view and when she did I felt my heart stop. She was dressed in overalls, stained from head to toe, and her hair was filthy. She carried an armful of twigs and broken branches. When she came up the walkway and looked at Harriet, it was with a depth of hatred I had never seen in a child.

"Go inside and wash your hands!" Harriet barked at Flora. She grabbed the girl by one ear and pulled her along toward the door.

"Harriet!" I stepped onto the porch and followed her inside before she could lock me out.

"What's the matter with you, Delphine?" She asked. "I haven't seen you in ages. Have you forgotten all about us?"

"I called but there was no answer."

"I've been too busy to talk on the phone." She nudged Flora toward the living room. "Didn't I tell you to put the kindling away? Go! Go, or I'll stuff you inside the chimney!"

If Flora had been a dog she would have bitten the woman's hand off. Obviously torn between following her nature and doing as she was told, she stomped into the living room and hurled the sticks and twigs against the fireplace. Then she darted around Harriet and fled upstairs.

"Little beast!" Harriet screamed after her. "Wait until Bill comes back. You'll apologize to me then, or you'll be sorry!"

I was so shocked I couldn't think of a thing to say.

"Delphine, I apologize," she said tearfully.

"Why is Flora gathering kindling? You have plenty of firewood."

"Bill thought it would help if she had a few chores, and I agree. You can see for yourself, she collected all of that on her own. At least it's a little progress, don't you think?"

"I don't understand."

Now she changed her tone.

"I'm under such a strain with Bill away all the time. I've been as good as I can be to that girl, but she's spiteful. She breaks things. She steals. All of my friends have abandoned me. I don't know what to do."

She sat down on the couch and wept. I sat opposite her and said, "Don't you think it's time for Flora to go home to her family?"

And just like that, she stopped crying. She wiped her face with a handkerchief, and then wiped off her lipstick.

"Haven't you done enough damage?" She said. "First you want me to educate the child. Then you want to take her away. If she's going to be educated we have to work through this phase. She has to learn to stop talking back and stop stealing, if she is to be civilized."

"I was wrong," I said. "Having her live with you isn't helping anything. And her family probably misses her."

"Not true," said Harriet. "Her father brings her back every time she runs away, and Bill pays him a reward every time. Her own father doesn't want her, and why would he? She's a lost cause."

"She ran away?"

"I've been telling you, Delphine: She's incorrigible. She's a criminal in the making. Someday she'll end up on death row if we can't change the course she's on. Can't you see that?"

"I don't know."

"Well, I know. I know I've lost my friends and devoted

myself to turning Flora's life around, and the thanks I get is that the people closest to me think I'm a monster. Even Kitty won't come to clean the house any more. I have to do it all myself, every single thing, and that horrible little girl torments me night and day!"

"If she can't be helped, and if she's as bad as that, you should send her away," I told her.

"No."

"If she's ruining your life," I said.

"No. I paid good money and I won't give up. She won't make me give up."

"I don't think she's trying to make you give up," I said as calmly as I could. "I think she just wants to go home."

"She doesn't have a home anymore."

"It might be bad, but if she wants to go back there we should let her."

"Delphine," she said. "Do you ever listen? There is no home for the girl except the one I've provided. One of Bill's associates bought that property."

"Where the Dempseys live?"

"Not any more. They never owned that lot. Never paid rent. They were squatters. Bill loaned this fellow he works with, Jim Crawford, the money to buy the whole kit and kaboodle."

I had never heard of such a thing. What struck me first was that William Knox would never think of such a thing on his own. He seemed far too busy. Only Harriet had time to plot against the girl in this way.

"But the Dempsey family's been there for ages."

"In a filthy two-room shack and a couple of tents? Jim had the whole place razed. Now we'll see where the little thief hides when she runs away. That ought to change her tune."

"What happened to the family?"

"Scattered to the winds, as far as I know. They weren't much of a family anyway. What kind of person sells his daughter for a hundred dollars?"

Harriet was right about Flora changing her tune. She got worse. According to Harriet she killed a neighbor's cat, a tabby that had never bothered a soul, and left it on Harriet's bed. Harriet made Bill punish the girl right before he left town for three weeks.

I'm not going to make excuses for myself. I know I should have done more to stop Harriet. Yet there was no legal way for me to take the girl away from her. Every time I spoke sharply Harriet threatened to tell the sheriff the names of those clients I had helped end a pregnancy. Although I might have been able to make the claim that I only prepared herbal tea for women in discomfort, I was shaken by the fact that Harriet had somehow ferreted out so much information about the women who came to me in desperation. I had no idea how much she knew about these women or how much damage she was willing to inflict on them just to punish me for disloyalty.

Finally, though, I have to own up to being afraid of the woman. It wasn't true that her friends shunned her because of Flora, although most of them didn't care for the girl. They were driven away by Harriet's obsession with taming Flora and commanding her respect at every turn. For reasons they never spelled out, they disliked Mr. Knox too.

These same women talked on the telephone about how they had always found Harriet's friendship too possessive and confining. She had a weird history, they said, but they also noted that she knew more about them than they knew about her. She was vicious, they said. She knew all about their views and their marriages. She had a terrible gift for inflicting pain and she relished the chance to witness a friend's disappointment. If she stumbled onto some bad news— as mild as Bonnie Cartwright's new dress not being ready in time for the dinner party with her husband's boss, or as serious as the x-ray Slim's doctor had taken— she would rush to deliver it, her hands and lips trembling with excitement.

So I held my tongue. I cleaned my house. I burned sage and said the words I had learned from Eve Alice, the words she had learned from her mother.

I put up new curtains and nailed rugs to the flimsy walls. I settled in for the long winter and I waited.

One night in early April there was a knock at the door. I was amazed to see Harriet. She wore no makeup and her eyes were bloodshot. She made me put on a coat and come with her. She drove through the winding back roads with the cool air and the scent of cedar streaming through the windows. She smoked a cigarette while she drove and she told me the story.

Flora had been sick. With her husband at home over the winter holidays Harriet claimed that she had longed for a family celebration, but the girl wasn't happy until she had ruined everything. Christmas was a disaster. First Flora couldn't keep any food down. She refused to join Harriet and William when the time came to open gifts. She broke glasses and windows. She set fire to a hearthrug.

When Flora continued to have an upset stomach off and on into the early spring, Harriet spent hours by her bedside feeding her broth and reading stories to make her recovery more pleasant. This is what she said, anyway.

Out of the blue Flora had told her a wicked story about William, who was now in Portland on business. No matter how many times Harriet threatened the girl, she would not take back her claim. I was warned not to believe her.

Fields and farmhouses and then forests thick with cedar and fir flashed by, as she drove. I shivered in the night air when Harriet described Flora's symptoms and her accusation. I didn't know what to believe. For one thing, I had never heard Flora put together more than three or four words at a time. I couldn't imagine her telling Harriet a story about anyone.

"She's the most devious person I've ever known," said Harriet.

"She's only just turned thirteen," I said.

"There! You see what a liar she is, Delphine? Her father is a liar, too, by the way. She was thirteen or fourteen when she came to live with us. Don't believe anything she says. All I want is for you to take a look at her and give me your verdict."

"If you're worried, we ought to call a doctor."

"Not after the story that little monster told me. No. You examine her. Then ask her to repeat what she said."

Flora's distended abdomen, the tenderness in her swollen breasts, her recurring nausea and sensitivity to odors and noises were just as Harriet described. All too obviously the girl was pregnant, I estimated five months along. The bruises on her arms and shoulders prompted me to make the first real threat I had ever spoken.

"Harriet, if you strike that girl one more time I'll call the sheriff on you, I swear. To hell with the consequences to me or anyone else."

We were standing in the living room. Harriet was smoking one cigarette after another. Flames crackled behind the fireplace screen. Outside a sullen moon cast its blue light over the fir and cedar and hemlock. The house felt remote and lonely in the cold woods.

"You don't know what I've been through," she said.

"No, but I can guess what she's been through. It's time to stop this."

"Delphine, I admit I was angry— very angry, and upset— when she told me she was with child. I imagined that she had met some boy the last time she ran away. But then when I questioned her and she said the father was my husband— I went wild. I hate lies! I know I was wrong. I'm sorry. It won't happen again."

"This is very serious. Harriet, look at me. This isn't about you or about me. She's going to have a baby in a few months. Whether your husband is the father or not, he has to stay away from her. Now what are you going to do?"

She bit her lower lip and stared into the fire. Then she

stubbed out her cigarette and turned to me.

"The answer is obvious, isn't it? I'm going to take care of her. This situation is my fault. I tried to turn her into something. I was terrible, and this is what comes of it. This is my punishment."

When she saw the expression on my face, she added: "How awful for Flora!"

For three months I visited Flora several times a week. Harriet still refused to let a doctor see her. This was her explanation:

"Delphine, I've seen doctors of one kind or another all of my life. You know what they're like. They're so arrogant, and most of the time they don't have a clue. They only repeat the symptoms you describe and write a prescription for some expensive treatment that makes you feel worse. Most of them hate women. We're guinea pigs to them, and you know it. All right, yes, I accept my responsibility for Flora's condition. God knows what really happened, but I'm sure what she said about Bill is a lie. It isn't true, Delphine, I swear to you. She wants to get even with me, and I can't say I blame her. I accept what I have to do, but I'm begging you not to tell anyone. Your life and mine and Bill's and Flora's will be ruined if you go to the sheriff. You know you're the best medical help she can get, and I promise I'll do everything possible to make things right. I won't leave her side. I'll hire someone to pick up groceries and to cook, and I won't let her suffer. She wouldn't get better help than that in a hospital, would she?"

I was about to speak when she added:

"If you called the authorities they would put her in one of those awful places and let her have her baby under terrible conditions. You know what I'm saying is true."

And as bad as it seems, I did. Harriet had created this mess for Flora, and I had helped her do it. Now it was up to us to turn things around, if that was possible.

On my orders Flora was bedridden for the rest of her pregnancy. We took every precaution. She was fed and bathed. She had backrubs and foot massages. We gave her red raspberry tea and slippery elm. Her sheets were changed every other day. Harriet read to her from a book of fairy tales.

Flora's favorite fairy tale was about a child in a faraway village stolen from its mother by fairies and replaced with a changeling. Flora would listen to this story the way she once tried to learn a simple task.

To most people in the village the changeling appeared to be the real child. Only its mother knew the difference. Everyone in the village believed the child's mother was mad.

The mother went to see a wise man and asked him what she should do. The wise man told her to accept the changeling as her own and give thanks, but she longed to hold her own child in her arms again.

The mother then went to a witch who lived in the forest and asked her for a spell to bring back her child. The witch agreed, but only if the mother would give her the real child upon its return.

No one else believed the mother. She grew thin and sick, mourning for her child, and yet no one would help her.

At last, in despair, she bundled the changeling in a blanket and threw it onto the fire in the hearth. When it caught the flames, and the smoke rose through the chimney, the fairies' spell was broken and the true child was magically returned to its mother's arms.

During the last weeks of Flora's pregnancy William Knox was nowhere to be seen. He had visited his wife infrequently throughout the winter and spring, and now he had settled in Olympia. He rented an apartment there. During one of their arguments on the telephone he informed Harriet that he had accepted a permanent position with the Department of Transportation in Washington, so they would not be returning to the east coast as originally planned.

I expected an outburst from Harriet over this news. Instead she called all of her friends and told them she had talked her husband into letting her stay in Skillute because she had fallen in love with the place. She told this tale again and again with an odd smile on her face. I wondered if this was how she convinced herself that things were all right.

With her husband she was suddenly as sweet as she could be on the telephone. She agreed to anything he wanted. She told him Flora was radiant with good health and everything was going to be fine. She was handling the situation, she said. She told him not to worry.

The night Flora went into labor, all of my fears came true. She was a slender girl, malnourished in childhood and small for her age. When the baby started to come, I realized the placenta had never moved into its proper position. It still rested in the lower part of the womb, partly covering the cervix opening.

As soon as the contractions started I ran for the telephone. There wasn't a sound on the line. I heard Flora screaming. From that second on my work was cut out for me.

With great effort we carried her to a cot Harriet had prepared in the kitchen. The girl kicked and thrashed so much we had to secure her with sheets tied to her arms and legs. When she couldn't get loose she growled and snapped her teeth at us, trying to bite. Nothing I said to her would calm her even a little bit. She had learned that grownup women were dangerous and she was in pain, so she might do anything.

The cervix was almost clear when Harriet turned to me and said:

"Whatever happens, you have to save the baby."

"The baby might live or might not," I told her. "Flora's young. She could have another baby."

Harriet said nothing to this.

Sweat ran from my face into my clothes. I had no choice but to try and shift the placenta, and this caused Flora to howl and cry so much I thought my heart would break. There was more blood than I'd ever seen before. It soaked the sheets and the cot mattress. It ran into our shoes and pooled under our feet.

With a scream as fierce as an animal's, Flora arched her back and let loose. The baby fell into my hands coated in scarlet gore. The afterbirth came quickly and ran down the sides of the cot.

The baby wasn't moving, wasn't breathing. I rubbed her tiny chest and shouted at Harriet to stop Flora's bleeding, but she never made a move to help the girl.

"Give it to me!" Harriet said, reaching for the newborn.

"She isn't breathing," I said.

"Give it to me! It's mine!"

I turned away from Harriet and Flora with the baby in my arms. Sweat blurred my vision. I soaked a cloth in water and sprinkled the infant's face, but she didn't blink.

Flora closed her eyes with a sigh. Her face was white, with purple shadows under her eyes. She shifted and reached, and then lay still. She never moved again.

"Give me the child," Harriet insisted. She reached toward me. "Giiiive!"

With a sputtering sound like water in a drain the baby drew her first breath. In my arms she shook, kicked, opened her mouth wide, and screamed.

Harriet reached out for the infant, and took her. She grinned and held the screaming baby in her arms. The woman I saw then was as close to a demon as anything in this world.

Nothing I'd lived through in Mount Coffin or anywhere else had prepared me for that night. Nothing can excuse what we did next.

Harriet bathed the infant and swaddled her in a blanket. We placed her in her crib and went downstairs to the kitchen where Flora's corpse lay twisted from its final convulsion. We lifted her from the cot and lay her onto a clean sheet on the floor.

I gathered up all of the bedclothes. Together we carried the cot mattress into the back yard. The warm night greeted us with the scent of evergreen. Overhead there was no break in the summer clouds and not a star to be seen anywhere.

We dug a pit out there between the trees, pushed back the leaves, made a ring of stones, and burned everything. When the fire died out we lay Flora's body down in the pit and covered it with lime from the garden shed, and then with dirt. I hoped this would be enough to keep her spirit quiet.

Harriet walked away. I called out to her but she ignored me.

So I knelt down on the damp soil. I took the leather pouch from around my neck, and I placed the tiny jawbone in the earth on top of Flora. As I pressed it into the earth, I said:

"Forgive us, Flora. Leave this world in peace. Let us go, now. Forgive me."

I was ashamed. I didn't know what to do except to carry on with the only life I had.

For three years I kept our secret. I watched Harriet raise Flora's child as her own. For three years I never contradicted Harriet's story that the girl had run off after stealing a pearl necklace and earrings. The little thief was probably in Canada by now, Harriet told everyone.

All the months Harriet had kept to herself that winter and spring now appeared to me in a new light. She had given herself over to nursing Flora, and stayed out of sight just enough in the months leading up to the baby's birth. She had been so cagey in the stories she told, and in her manner and her dress, that some people actually believed her. Others wondered, but they didn't wonder enough to do more than ignore Harriet's party invitations. Life went on as it had before. No one missed Flora. After a time people even forgot her first name.

Meanwhile the baby grew stronger. Mr. and Mrs. William Knox named her Ella, and people said she favored her father. This was true. She had his dark hair, his smile, and his violet eyes.

In temper, though, something else began to shine through. Call it a streak of danger or a thread of madness. Neighbors sometimes caught a glimpse of the tot clutching her mother's hand, dragging her along while the woman tried to shop or carry on a conversation. Once Harriet leaned down to button Ella's sweater and the girl slapped her in the mouth, cutting her lips and causing the blood to run down her chin.

'Little hellion' people said, and not always with a smile. There were women, Bonnie Cartwright among them, who watched their own children like hawks whenever Ella was around. They never said that she frightened them. Maybe they suspected that saying it out loud might make their fears come true. In any case, Harriet's came true.

Ella was three and a half when Harriet discovered that she was pregnant. Now she put on weight and redecorated the house, to which William added a nursery and a back porch. House proud, planting tulips in the garden and chatting with her few remaining girlfriends on the telephone every day, Harriet spent less and less time with Ella. She left the child in the care of the cleaning woman, an elderly spinster who sometimes tied Ella to her highchair to keep her out of the way.

One night I woke from a dream I couldn't recall and lay in my bed with my heart racing. I thought I heard Eve Alice talking, but I couldn't make out the words.

There was a knock at the screen door. I put on my robe, went to the kitchen, and looked out.

The man nodded at me in greeting. He still wore a loose fitting shirt and trousers, with a watch chain stretched across a vest with several pockets. He pulled the wide-brimmed straw hat from his head and held it in both hands, and waited until I spoke.

"Can I help you?" I asked.

"Thank you kindly," he said. "I would be ever so grateful."

His accent was the same as I remembered, with a slight lilt at the end of each sentence. He smiled.

"Well," I said. "How can I help you?"

"Gracious lady," he said. "I believe your help is needed elsewhere. There is the child to consider."

I ran back to my room and dressed as fast as I could. When I returned to the screen door the man was gone.

I drove along the same back roads I had taken years before to reach Harriet's house. The trip took me past the old Dempsey place. Nothing of the cabin with the corrugated tin roof remained except the front steps. They sat there in the middle of the lot, still empty and silent in the pale moonlight. No one had built there in all the time since Harriet's friend had burned down the Dempsey's home.

I drove on, and the Chevy made good time. A mile before I reached my destination I smelled it, winding its wicked path through the Douglas fir, sharp and unmistakable: Fire.

By the time I reached the cottage the smoke was thick and rolling up from the ground in black waves. It made my eyes water and I started to cough. I pushed through the gate in the front yard and saw the smoke streaming in columns from all of the windows, the bedrooms and the nursery. From upstairs there was a shattering of glass and everything seemed to roil and tumble in the copper flames.

There in the frame of the front door, sitting among the charred bits of wallpaper wafting through from the hall, was Ella. Her face was smudged with ash and her gown was torn.

I ran to the child and swept her into my arms. I wrapped her in my coat and hurried away from that place. I walked back the way I had come, through the garden gate. I put the child on the backseat and I drove like a demon away from that inferno. The heat and fury climbed up into the night behind us, burning a hole right through the canopy of blackened cedar and fir.

For three days the child slept and I couldn't wake her. I gave her water by ringing a damp cloth into her mouth. I sat by her side and spoke to her all day. I slept beside her all night. When she finally opened her eyes, she didn't know me but she didn't seem to mind having me nearby.

She never cried. She never asked where she was. She didn't know her name or where she came from. She followed me wherever I went. She laughed when I laughed and slept when I slept.

I taught her to keep quiet in the bedroom whenever women came to me for a consultation. Later I taught her many other things, all of the remedies I knew from my grandmother, the only other woman I loved, the only other person in my life who was true and kind.

Harriet and William were given a Christian memorial along with their unborn child. It was assumed that Ella died with them. There were few remains. When the fire caught the garage the cars caused an explosion. Debris was found in the woods from time to time, years later.

More people moved to and from Skillute for one reason or another. I went on with my life, which now had a greater purpose thanks to the child I had saved. I gave you the name Marietta because it had a joyful sound. When I introduced you to people at last, and said you were my niece, no one questioned my word.

Everything seemed all right until you started school. That's when I knew there was the possibility of both light and darkness in you. If another child spoke kindly to you I could see your soul come alive, and you responded with deep generosity. But whenever someone crossed your path and caused you pain or caused the other children you liked to suffer in some way, there was trouble. I don't mean you set out to harm anyone, I don't believe that. But in one way or another, the people who hurt you came to harm.

This is why I urged you to be calm and to think before you speak. This is why I watched you closely and taught you the more innocent incantations and remedies I knew. I don't think you would injure anyone on purpose, but your heart is strong and you have a powerful sense of justice that calls out to the world around you.

This is why I've always asked you to be gentle, and to be solitary when other people disappoint you. Please remember that you have never disappointed me. You have been as good to me as a loving and devoted daughter. My life has been better with you. I have known comfort and kindness in my old age because of you.

Now I can see that keeping you with me has made you lonely. I didn't know it before, but I've seen how bashfully you smile at the slightest kind word from a stranger. Now the danger comes right to our doorstep, and I'm afraid I won't be here to protect you much longer. I've written these pages as faithfully as possible, so that you can see all that I've seen, and be ready.

I don't expect you to understand all that I've done, Marietta. I only hope you know what I mean when I say: This is your time. Forgive me.

Delphine Dodd
Skillute, Washington
1975

Acknowledgements

Thanks to my husband Cory James Herndon for making everything possible. Thanks to Kate Jonez for editorial wizardry and Suzanne Morrison for notes, encouragement, and expert advice. Thanks to Lucy Taylor, Angel Leigh McCoy, Joe Mullenix and Jessica Moore for encouragement, and to the judges of the Shirley Jackson Awards for including *Knock Knock* on the 2011 shortlist. Most of all, thanks to the readers who have taken *Knock Knock* to heart.

Thank you to everyone who supported this project with their donations: Scott Gable, Andrew Deutsch, Anna Murchison, SHAUN, Deniece Bleha, Jessica Moore, Constance Wang, Phil Hickes, joemullenix, Steve and Anne Williams, William McDermott, Penelope Levy, Ripley Patton, Cindy Flanary, Chris Diani, Greg Lyle-Newton, Juhana Jaaksi, Angel Leigh McCoy, Sheri Holman, Jason Rinn, Heidi Searing, Shannon Herndon, Maria Glanz, and Derek Sunshine.

Readers interested in learning more about the Pacific Northwest will enjoy Jack Nisbet's excellent history *Visible Bones: Journeys Across Time in the Columbia River Country* and *Emerald City: An Environmental History of Seattle* by Matthew Klingle, as well as Anne Cameron's collection of northwest coast Native myths, *Daughters of Copper Woman*. These fascinating books, along with numerous articles and sites online, served as references and resources for *Knock Knock* and *Delphine Dodd*.

About the Author

Rated by Black Static book critic Peter Tennant as "one of the most interesting and original writers to emerge in recent years," S.P. Miskowski has written short stories published in *Supernatural Tales, Horror Bound Magazine, Identity Theory, The Absent Willow Review, Fine Madness, Other Voices*, and the anthology *Detritus*. Her work has received two Swarthout prizes and two National Endowment for the Arts Fellowships. Her supernatural thriller *Knock Knock* was shortlisted for a Shirley Jackson Award and the first in a series of three Knock Knock-related novellas, *Delphine Dodd*, is a finalist for a Shirley Jackson Award in 2013. Raised in Decatur, Georgia, Miskowski now lives in California with her husband, author Cory J. Herndon. You can contact the author and comment on this book or *Knock Knock* on our Facebook page or at the author's blog:

http://d-o-cat.blogspot.com/

About the Cover Illustrator

The cover design and illustration for *Delphine Dodd* are by Russell Dickerson. You can find more of his work at Darkstorm Creative:

http://www.darkstormcreative.com/

Printed in Great Britain
by Amazon